ARCHVILLAIN

ARCHVILLAIN

by **BARRY LYGA**

SCHOLASTIC PRESS · NEW YORK

Library of Congress Cataloging-in-Publication Data

Lyga, Barry.
    Archvillain / Barry Lyga. — 1st ed.
        p. cm.
    Summary: Twelve-year-old Kyle Camden develops greater mental agility and superpowers during a plasma storm that also brings Mighty Mike, an alien, to the town of Bouring, but while each does what he thinks is best, Kyle is labeled a villain and Mike a hero.
    ISBN 978-0-545-19649-9
    [1. Superheroes – Fiction. 2. Extraterrestrial beings – Fiction. 3. Good and evil – Fiction. 4. Science fiction.] I. Title.
    PZ7.L97967Arc 2010
    [Fic] – dc22

                                                                    2010005291

10 9 8 7 6 5 4 3 2 1   10 11 12 13 14

Printed in the U.S.A.   23
First edition, October 2010

The text type was set in Sabon
Book design by Christopher Stengel

For my brother, Eric –
my very first audience

Where Were You When the Stars Fell Down?

In the days since a massive meteor shower lit up the night sky over Bouring, residents have been asking one another, "Where were you when the stars fell down?" It's a question that has set abuzz a town whose motto is "Bouring — It's not Boring!"

Lacey Clark, owner of Clark's Bakery on Wayne Street, was closing up her shop that night. "I was just locking the door when I saw a bright flash of light to the east," she told BouringRecord.com. "I sort of stood there in shock, watching."

"It went yellow, then white, then yellow again," said Paul West, who was working on a utility pole on Allen Road at the time of the meteor shower. "I was up pretty high, so I had a good view of the whole thing. I swear, it was like a curtain of light or like seeing the stars fall down."

Best estimates place the meteor shower's landing point at or near the Bouring Middle School athletic fields and the nearby Bouring Water Tower. The shower lit up the entire town for a period of two minutes, causing many to run or drive to the fields.

When they arrived, however, they did not find a smoking crater or other evidence of meteors. In fact, according to astronomers, the meteors all burned up in Earth's atmosphere before hitting the ground. This burning, astronomers say, is what caused the bright flashes of light.

Of course, something else was found at the scene when all those people arrived: a young boy, approximately twelve years of age, who had apparently stumbled onto the scene. Suffering from amnesia, that boy — named Mike by the doctors who took care of him — is now in the care of a local foster couple.

It's been four days and we want to know, Bouring: Where were *you* when the stars fell down? Tell us in the comments below!

from the top secret journal of
Kyle Camden (deciphered):

"Where were you when the stars fell down?" Idiots!

The stars didn't "fall down." Stars can't *fall down!*
Stars aren't little pinpoints of light up in the sky. They're
gigantic balls of superheated gases. They're basically
enormous nuclear bombs. If a star — any star *— came*
within fifty million miles of the planet, the entire solar
system would be realigned by tidal gravitational
forces and all life on Earth would end. So nothing
"fell down."

These people should do their research.

Second of all, it wasn't a meteor shower. It was a
focused curtain of supercooled plasma. That's why there
was no physical evidence of a meteor shower.

How do I know this? I was there.

I was in the field that night. No one knows this.
I watched the plasma storm as it fell; it was extra-
ordinary.

I don't remember much else. Certainly not this
"Mike" the article mentions. I stumbled home, then col-
lapsed into bed.

The next thing I knew, I woke up at home days
later. . . .

CHAPTER
ONE

Kyle Camden did not like his mother fussing over him, as she did now. "That was just the worst flu I've ever seen," she told Kyle as she fluffed his pillow and urged him to eat the chicken soup she'd delivered on a tray.

Kyle also did not like chicken soup.

Correction: Kyle did not like his *mother's* chicken soup. The broth was watery and flavorless. Kyle could make better chicken soup without even using a chicken. That's how bad a cook his mother was. At least she kept trying, though. He had to give her points for persistence. If she kept trying, maybe someday she would get it right. Kyle figured there was a fifty-fifty chance.

"I'm fine, Mother," he told her. Kyle knew that he hadn't had the flu: He had witnessed something amazing the other night, out in the field by the school. And even though the local newspapers and websites apparently had never heard of that exotic practice known as "fact-checking," at least they allowed him to catch up with what had happened since that night he'd stumbled home, delirious.

The plasma curtain had done something to Kyle. He realized it as soon as he woke up and logged on to the London *Times* website for his morning ritual — solving the *Times* crossword puzzle. (American crosswords had long ago proven too easy for him — the British ones were tough.) Instead of taking ten minutes, like it used to, Kyle had solved the toughest crossword puzzle in all of *two* minutes.

Kyle had always been smart. *Really* smart. Much smarter than his parents, in fact. Sometimes he felt a little twinge of guilt about this. His parents were nice enough people, he supposed. A bit dull. But they were kindhearted and they tried hard, which counted for *something*, right? Still, it had always been frustrating to be a genius in a family of . . . non-geniuses.

Kyle didn't mention his ramped-up brainpower to his parents. At twelve years old, he already knew how important it was to keep his own business secret. It would remain between him and Lefty, the fat New Zealand rabbit who lived in a cage in Kyle's room. Lefty was snowy white all over except for a tiny patch of brown fur on his left front paw. The rabbit placidly observed everything with his pink-red eyes as though he knew a secret he would never, ever tell.

"I don't want you on the Internet," Kyle's mother said, having finished fluffing the pillow and placing it behind Kyle's head. "I want you to rest."

Kyle rolled his eyes. "Mother, I need to catch up on what's been happening while I was sick. And I need to catch up on my schoolwork." That last part was a lie. Shortly after waking up, Kyle had sat up in bed with his laptop and done his missed schoolwork in an hour. Then, just to be safe, he'd also done the next two weeks' worth of work. That had taken another hour. Superintelligence could be convenient.

Once his mother left, Kyle immediately slid his laptop out from under his bed. Then he opened the window. It was cool outside, but Mom had the heat cranked up to "Volcanic." Kyle sighed with relief at the breeze.

Lefty started tugging on the bars of his cage, demanding a treat, so Kyle shook a couple of bits of dried papaya into the cage. Lefty scampered over and devoured them.

"It's been a strange few days, hasn't it, Lefty?"

The last thing he remembered after the plasma storm was stumbling home, his vision blurry, his head pounding as if someone had used it for a drum solo. His parents thought he had the flu and kept him in bed for days. Now he understood that his exposure to the plasma had changed his body and he'd needed all that rest to recover.

But recovery time was over.

His father poked his head into the room. "Hey, there, sport! Now that you're feeling better, you can go to school in the morning!"

Great.

CHAPTER TWO

Since all of his schoolwork was done, Kyle spent his last night of freedom thinking of ways to help his parents. They were nice enough people, and it wasn't their fault that they were, well, "intellectually ungifted" was probably the kindest way to put it.

His mother worked in the mayor's office, but she never really complained about work, so Kyle figured she was pretty happy there. But her cooking . . . *ugh*! She definitely needed help in that department. Best of all, helping Mom in the kitchen would help Kyle, too, because he could finally eat something that didn't make him sick to his stomach. It was a win-win scenario, the best kind.

And Dad! Dad was always complaining about his weight. (How he could gain so much weight eating Mom's cooking was a mystery that Kyle feared even his newly enhanced brainpower could not solve.) He would help his father lose weight and get in shape. Excellent!

"I am probably the best son in the history of sons," Kyle told Lefty very seriously. Lefty cocked a red eye at

Kyle and twitched his nose, which Kyle chose to interpret as agreement.

A little while later, he found his parents in their usual spot — on the sofa, in front of the TV. Kyle had little use for TV; most of it was dumb. His parents, though, were hooked on it. They had complicated schedules to determine which shows to watch on which days, which ones would be recorded and watched later, and which ones would be put off until the DVD came out.

"Hey, guys," Kyle said, holding up two DVDs he'd just made on his computer, "I have something for you."

"Can it wait until the commercial, sport?" Dad asked, his eyes glued to the screen.

"I guess."

Kyle flounced into a chair that didn't directly face the TV and waited. And waited. And waited. Was there *ever* going to be a commercial?

Finally, the commercial break came. Kyle jumped up and waved the DVDs in front of his parents' faces. "I made these for you. To help you."

Mom eyed the DVDs suspiciously, as though she'd never before seen this strange, futuristic technology. "Is this one of your pranks, honey?"

"What? No!" Kyle was offended by the very suggestion. He was trying to *help*!

Kyle was on his way to becoming the World's Greatest Prankster. His parents, his schoolmates, his teachers, even the local police — all had been his victims at one point or another.

"Victims" wasn't really the best way to put it, though. Kyle preferred to think of them as "beneficiaries." His pranks weren't supposed to hurt people. They were supposed to teach people to lighten up. It wasn't *his* fault if they rarely learned the lesson.

"Look," he explained, "I used some videos and instructional websites that I found online and I assembled them into a sequence designed to maximize knowledge intake in your frontal lobes, okay? Very simple. Then I accelerated the pace of the information display, optimized to your individual neural networks and optical capabilities so that the data can be presented and assimilated subliminally. Pretty cool, huh?"

His parents stared at him. Then they stared at each other. Then, for variety, they stared at him again.

"So it *is* a prank," Dad said.

"No! No. Look, it's just . . ." Kyle took a deep breath and dumbed it down for them. "These are like instructional videos, only really fast and made especially for you." He could tell he was losing them. "They run at high speed. Hours compressed into minutes."

"Then how are we supposed to learn from them?" Mom asked.

"Your brain will pick up on the information without you even trying," Kyle told her. "Look, just trust me, okay? Try them out. Mom, here's yours." He held it out to her. "It's a whole series of cooking lessons, so that you can, uh . . ." He struggled with a diplomatic way of saying "not suck at cooking." "Well, it's so you can cook."

"But I already know how to cook, honey."

Kyle decided to deal with her later. He turned to his father. "Dad, I made this one for you. It's a complete workout routine and weight-loss regimen."

Dad took the DVD and turned it over in his hands, then chuckled. "Well, I appreciate the thought, sport, but it's not that easy. You can't just watch something faster and lose weight faster."

Kyle growled a bit. "That's not how it works, Dad. You watch it faster to *learn* it faster and *then* —"

"Oh, look, it's back on!" Mom cried. "Move, Kyle."

Kyle considered staying between them and their beloved TV, but it was useless. They didn't get it. In fact, Dad had already put his DVD on the end table . . . and was using it as a coaster for his drink.

Kyle stomped off to his bedroom and kicked the aluminum trash can next to his desk before he could remember how much it hurt every time he did that.

But this time, not only did it *not* hurt . . .

The trash can shot up off the floor and went sailing right through Kyle's window! Fortunately, the window was still open, so the glass was safe. That screen, though, would never be the same again. It was a shredded mess.

Kyle stood perfectly still and silent for a moment, staring at it. Lefty seemed to be staring, too. Kyle went over to the window and peered through the gaping hole in the screen. The trash can had landed at the very edge of the Camdens' backyard, dented and mangled almost beyond recognition.

"Well," Kyle said. He turned to Lefty. "*That*'s interesting."

CHAPTER
THREE

In the morning, before he had to leave for school, Kyle slipped outside and retrieved what used to be his trash can. The ground around the spot where it had landed was indented, and the grass even looked a little singed. The trash can itself was . . .

Well, the trash can was trash now.

He must have been really, *really* angry at his parents last night when he'd kicked it.

Back inside, Kyle choked down his mother's oatmeal (how could she mess up *oatmeal?*), grabbed his things for school, and dashed outside to catch the bus as it pulled up to the end of his driveway.

A cheer went up from the kids on the bus as Kyle stepped on the top stair. Someone started chanting, "CAM-den! CAM-den!" and soon the whole bus joined in. Kyle held up his hands to quiet them, then made his way to the back of the bus, where his usual reserved seat awaited him. Along the way, he was slapped on the back and high-fived as he moved down the aisle.

After being out sick for so long, it felt great to be back among his friends. Kyle was the most popular kid at Bouring Middle School, which made sense, since he had also been the most popular kid at Bouring Elementary School.

"Good to have you back, man!" James called.

"Thanks!" Kyle replied, grinning.

"You feeling okay? You doing all right?" Ellen asked, concerned.

"Never better," Kyle told her, and swung into his seat. "Never better."

The bus driver let the brakes go — they whined and shrieked — and then the bus lurched forward. Kyle leaned back. Already, the kids who sat in the seats in front of him had turned around to ask him questions: Was it true he'd had an incurable disease . . . and then cured it himself? (No. Good story, though.) Was the whole sickness thing just a bluff, a way of getting out of school? (Faking illness to get out of school? Puh-lease! Anyone could do that!) Did he spend his time at home planning his next awesome prank?

Hmm. Well, no. He hadn't. He'd been really, really out of it. But he didn't want people to think he was off his game, so he just grinned like he had a secret. Everyone started high-fiving one another. Kyle's pranks were legendary among the people of Bouring, especially the kids. That's because Kyle didn't just zing people his own age —

he zinged the adults, too, usually in such a way that no one could actually *prove* it had been Kyle.

Even the local sheriff, Maxwell Monroe, wasn't safe. Last year, Kyle had hacked into the Bouring police band in order to broadcast his Prankster Manifesto. The Prankster Manifesto was simple and to the point:

THE PRANKSTER MANIFESTO
BY KYLE CAMDEN

1. PEOPLE ARE FOOLISH.
2. SERIOUS PEOPLE ARE DOUBLY FOOLISH. ESPECIALLY PEOPLE IN AUTHORITY: PARENTS, TEACHERS, ETC.
3. PRANKS SHOW PEOPLE HOW FOOLISH THEY ARE.
4. IT'S GOOD TO SHOW PEOPLE HOW FOOLISH THEY ARE BECAUSE THEN THEY STOP ACTING SO SERIOUS.
5. WHEN THEY STOP ACTING SO SERIOUS, THEY CAN UNDERSTAND THE TRUTH.
6. WHICH IS THAT THEY'RE FOOLISH.
7. KYLE CAMDEN IS ALLOWED TO BE SERIOUS BECAUSE HE'S NOT FOOLISH.

It was a pretty simple manifesto. It only took a minute to broadcast it. But Sheriff Monroe acted as though Kyle had committed high treason. (As if the Bouring police band was ever used for anything other than the cops calling one another for coffee and doughnut runs.) Kyle's parents had taken away his computer and his TV and grounded him for weeks after that. He had learned an important lesson: From then on, he operated in secret.

He had only shared the news of his new boosted intellect with Lefty, who wouldn't be blabbing to anyone, obviously. And, of course, he had recorded the information in a new cipher he'd invented for his top secret journal.

(Kyle kept a written journal, as opposed to one on the computer. He had a very simple reason for this: Kyle's business was his own and no one else's, and after all, it's impossible to hack paper.)

The bus jerked to a halt, its brakes wheezing like an old man who has run a marathon, and Kyle's best friend, Mairi MacTaggert, got on. Her eyes lit up when she saw Kyle, and she walked quickly to his seat.

"Can I sit here?"

"I was saving it for you," Kyle said.

Mairi smiled, her eyes shining green under her mane of red hair. She slid into the seat next to him.

"I was worried about you, Kyle. That was the longest you've ever been sick. And when I called, your parents said they didn't know what was wrong with you."

There was no one on the planet smart enough to know what had happened to Kyle. Except for Kyle, of course, and even he wasn't sure.

"I'm fine. They worry too much."

"You didn't miss much in school. In case you were worried."

Kyle laughed. "I bet it was pretty boring without me around."

Mairi considered. "Well, it was *quiet*, I'll tell you that. No remote-controlled mice. No purple water in the drinking fountains. No random burping noises from the computers."

"No one ever proved I did any of that stuff."

"Oh, *I know*," Mairi said airily. "So I guess it's just a coincidence that *nothing* like that happened while you were out sick?"

Kyle shrugged, which was really the only safe response. He didn't want to lie to Mairi. She was the only person who ever really understood him in the entire town of Bouring. She was the only one who never wanted anything from him.

Sure, he was popular . . . but that popularity came with a price. "Hey, Kyle," a kid would say, "can you pull a cool prank on my mom?" Or, "Can you help me get back at my big sister?" But Mairi never asked anything of Kyle. She just liked hanging out with him.

"Hey, remember the time you rewired the loud-speakers so that the principal sounded like Dora the Explorer?" Mairi asked.

That had been a classic from third grade. "That was a long time ago. I've matured since then."

"Sure you have."

Having someone as your friend for as long as you

17

can remember is great — but the downside is that they know everything about you. Mairi had actually been present the day Kyle decided to embark on a life of pranukster-ing. It was back in first grade, when a group of middle school actors visited the elementary school to perform their own version of *The Emperor's New Clothes*. Kyle had been captivated by the story of an arrogant, self-important monarch who was so impervious to common sense that he walked around naked, convinced he was wearing fine clothes.

As he watched the play, Mairi had leaned over to him and whispered, "It's just like real life!"

Even that young, they'd both already recognized that many adults took themselves too seriously and needed to be taken down a peg or two. Or ten. The teacher who always said "supposably" instead of "supposedly." The principal who walked the halls with his shirttail sticking out of his fly. The lunch monitor who couldn't tell the difference between a stalk of asparagus . . . and a green bean. They were surrounded by clueless people.

Mairi thought it was funny, but even in the first grade, Kyle — already a genius — knew that it was deadly serious. And a problem. Even though it would be more than a year before he actually wrote it down, the Prankster Manifesto was born that day.

Now that he once again sat on the bus with Mairi, the world made at least a little sense. He tried to stay casual, but he couldn't help it — he was happy to see her. Even though Mairi didn't always appreciate Kyle's pranks (the ones she knew about, that is), she also never hassled him about them.

"Are you still doing the Astronomy Club thing?"

The Bouring Astronomy Club was holding its monthly stargazing event in a couple of weeks. Mairi and Kyle had always gone to them together and he didn't see why that would change now. "Of course."

"It's your turn to bring the snacks."

"I know. I'm not an idiot." That was more true than ever now.

Mairi punched Kyle in the shoulder. "No one said you were an idiot, you idiot."

Kyle grinned back at her, but inside, he was suddenly cold and worried. Mairi was pretty tough; she had a decent punch.

But when she'd punched him just now . . . he hadn't felt a thing.

By the time they got to school, Kyle was still thinking about that punch. Had Mairi pulled her punch, worried about hurting him since he'd been sick? That made sense.

At school, he'd barely gotten off the bus when his Great Nemesis swooped into view.

"Hello, Kyle!" his Great Nemesis burbled.

"Hello, Great Nemesis." Kyle gritted his teeth.

"Oh, Kyle! Are you still calling me that?"

Melissa Masterton. Bouring Middle School's guidance counselor. She had been Bouring Elementary School's guidance counselor and then transferred to the middle school at the same time Kyle started. He was convinced she was stalking him. Isn't that what a Great Nemesis would do?

Ms. Masterton was always trying to help Kyle. This was particularly annoying because Kyle didn't *need* any help. Ms. Masterton called what she did "channeling your energies." As if Kyle were a raging river that needed a dam.

She also didn't seem to understand that Kyle really, genuinely did not like her. She thought he was kidding about the "Great Nemesis" stuff.

"You've been out of school for a week," she went on. "I want to make sure you don't need any help getting back on your feet."

He glared at Ms. Masterton, who beamed down at him like a deranged grandmother. Her eyes had blue eyeliner all around them and her face was thick with pasty makeup. Kyle wondered how many pounds of makeup she went through in a year. It had to be a lot.

"I'm on my feet just fine," he told her. "Standing up and everything."

"A long illness can be difficult, especially for someone as bright and competitive as you are," she babbled. "You might be afraid that you'll never catch up."

Ha! Kyle had done his missing work and more. He started calculating her makeup poundage, just to make the time pass.

"So I just want you to know that I talked to your teachers and they're all willing to give you as much time as you need to get acclimated." She paused. "Acclimate is a word that means —"

Become accustomed to a new climate or new conditions, Kyle thought, still calculating. In lipstick alone, she probably used twenty pounds a year. Eyeliner weighed less, but she probably used more of it, so figure another twenty pounds there.

"And I just know you'll do great!" Ms. Masterton went on, and then did the most horrible thing a Great Nemesis could do: She leaned down and hugged Kyle, right there in broad daylight!

"Now go on inside and don't be afraid to come to my office if you need to!"

Kyle broke away from her, grateful that no one had seen that little display.

Fifty pounds, he settled on. Fifty pounds, ten ounces, to be exact. That's how much makeup Ms. Masterton went through in a year.

That's a kindergartner's weight in makeup!

CHAPTER
FOUR

Once he got inside the school, Kyle realized the cold, hard truth: He was in middle school. He had an intellect the size of a moon and he was trapped in the sixth grade. The boredom would crush him like an egg and leave a gross, gooey mess. In truth, "bored" was too small and too normal a word to describe what he felt. School had never been much of a challenge for him, but now he was so smart that his old smartness looked like stupidity, and that made his boredom come alive like a giant wearing steel-toed boots, crushing everything in its path.

He occupied his mind with other things instead. Like: How had his intelligence been boosted? Did things besides his brain get changed by the radiation? Did that explain his deadly trash-can-kicking prowess? And his sudden ability to ignore a punch from Mairi MacTaggert?

Then he remembered something from the article about the "stars falling down" — there had been someone *else* in the field that night. Another kid Kyle's age.

That was strange because Kyle had no memory of any-one else being there, but BouringRecord.com said there had been. Maybe he could go find this kid and compare notes. . . .

The idea of needing help from someone else didn't sit well with Kyle. Not at all.

Lunchtime helped Kyle forget his troubles. Kids fought over the opportunity to sit at his table. Kyle tried his best to keep the peace, but he had to admit that it was kind of cool to have everyone want to be that close to him.

"All right!" he said finally, when he judged that Mr. Hathaway, the lunch monitor, was going to intervene. "That's enough, you guys. You, you, and you" — he pointed — "can sit here. The rest of you will have to wait until tomorrow."

"But there's one more seat!" someone complained.

"I'm saving that one," Kyle told him, and glanced over to the end of the lunch line, where Mairi had just paid for her lunch. Kyle had brown-bagged it. (He made his own lunches, so they were tasty. He hadn't let his mother near his lunch bag since fourth grade. It was just a matter of survival.)

Lunch was, as usual, terrific. No one spoke as Kyle held forth on all sorts of topics, including — to the amusement of everyone — his rough calculation of the Great Nemesis's makeup poundage. The table roared with such laughter that Kyle worried it might be *too* much. Kids from other tables looked over with sad envy. Even Mr. Hathaway looked like he wished he could be in on the fun.

After lunch, Kyle headed outside with everyone else for recess. It was a cool autumn day and the sun was a solid, bright disc. Sides were chosen for basketball, with Kyle deciding not to play. He had never been good at sports, probably because he'd never really put his mind to it. While other kids had kicked soccer balls or swung bats or dribbled or whatever else athletes did, Kyle had been in his room, planning his next awesome prank. He didn't have anything against sports — he just couldn't be bothered.

"Are you sure you don't want to play?" Mairi asked. "You can be on my team."

"Nah, go have fun," he told her. "I'm still not a hundred percent."

Mairi's mouth turned down in a worried frown. "Did you come back too soon?" she asked in a very motherly tone of voice that almost made Kyle burst out laughing.

"I'm good. I'll watch."

He stood off to one side and tuned out the game as it went on. He had more important things to think about. Like that web account, which claimed that there had been another kid in the field the night of the plasma storm. Why couldn't Kyle remember that? He started to wonder if maybe he should swallow his pride and find this "Mike" kid.

But no. He couldn't do that. He couldn't let anyone know he'd been in the field that night. The only reason he'd been there at all was because the Bouring High School Hawks were going to be playing a visiting team on the middle school field the next day. The high school field was being resodded, so they were going to use Bouring Middle's. There was a large water tower just north of the field, and Kyle thought it would be a great prank to rig the tower to douse both teams just before halftime. (If he managed to soak the crowd, too, that would just be a bonus.)

Bouring, after all, took its football team far too seriously. Therefore, he had to show them how silly that was. Drenching the team and turning the football field into a mud-wrestling pit would do the trick.

So, no, telling anyone where he'd been was *not* —

"Heads up!" someone shouted, just as the basketball careened through the air and smacked Kyle in the face.

"I'm so sorry! So sorry! So sorry!" a kid yelled, running toward Kyle, his arms pumping.

Kyle blinked and bent over to pick up the ball. He hadn't felt anything when the ball slammed into him. And it had slammed *hard*. He'd had no time to react at all.

He tossed the ball to the kid headed his way.

Mairi came running over. "Are you okay?"

"I'm fine."

"Didn't it hurt? It looked like it hurt."

Hurt? Oh, right. Getting hit in the face with a ball was supposed to hurt.

"A little," he lied. "Ow. It sort of mostly bounced off my forehead."

Mairi gave him that motherly look, but then someone shouted for her from the basketball court, so she jogged back, leaving Kyle to wonder why — suddenly — he couldn't be hurt.

CHAPTER
FIVE

At home that night, Kyle dawdled over his dinner. For once, it wasn't because he was trying to avoid eating. He was too occupied thinking about what had happened that day. Had he somehow become immune to pain? Had the plasma storm done more than simply boost his intellect into the stratosphere? Had it also changed him physically?

"You're quiet tonight, sport!" Dad said.

"Just thinking."

"About what, honey?" Mom asked.

Kyle sighed. His parents had rarely been helpful in the past, but he figured maybe he owed it to them to give them one more shot.

"Well," he said, "I sort of feel like I'm going through some changes. . . ."

His parents shot worried looks at each other.

"Uh, I see," Dad said, clearing his throat. "You know, we've talked about some of this in the past, but I guess . . . You know, at your age, your body is going to go through changes and you're going to get feelings —"

"Not that, Dad!" Oh, man! Kyle did *not* want to have *that* talk!

But Kyle's dad took his parenting business very seriously. "I know it's embarrassing to talk about, but I think you need to hear it. So, when you start to get older, chemicals in your body . . ."

Kyle put his head down on the table and tried to block out his father's voice as Dad told him things he already knew and didn't want to hear about again. Especially from his father. At the dinner table. With his mother sitting right there.

Eventually, his dad had mercy and wrapped up the speech, allowing Kyle to escape to his bedroom, confident that his parents were, indeed, totally useless in this case.

"I could learn more talking to you, Lefty," he told the rabbit. Lefty had no opinion on the subject but clearly wanted something sweet to eat. Kyle gave him a yogurt drop and flopped on his bed to think.

When scientists had theories, they tested them. That's what Kyle needed to do.

He imagined stabbing himself with knives and dropping heavy weights on his feet, but that seemed pretty radical. What if he was only invulnerable to basketballs and girls?

He had to try *something*!

After darkness fell, long after he was supposed to be asleep, Kyle crept silently out of bed and opened his bedroom window. His room looked out on the backyard and a dense growth of woods — no one would see him.

"You keep your mouth shut about this, Lefty," Kyle said. Lefty yawned, showing big white teeth.

When he'd been younger, Kyle had jumped out of his bedroom window. It wasn't that far to the ground, so he'd never been in any real danger, but it *had* hurt when he landed. It hurt enough that he'd cried out and his parents had come running. He'd been grounded for two weeks after that little stunt.

So he knew he could survive the jump. The only question was: Would it hurt?

He bit his lip, gazing down at the ground.

Then, before he could change his mind, Kyle launched himself out the window.

And didn't fall.

Kyle hung suspended in the air just outside his window, floating in the dark. He was so shocked that for a moment, he thought he'd landed on his head and was hallucinating.

But no. He could fly.

He. Could. *Fly!*

With a thought, he angled his body, arching upward, gliding through the air like a fish in water. It was as though he'd been doing it his whole life.

The air rushed over him! The night sky beckoned!

He twisted in the air and flew higher, over the house, moving quickly. He was wearing dark clothes, so he didn't think anyone would notice him, if anyone happened to glance in this direction at this time of night.

Kyle flew to the outskirts of town, to an abandoned coal mine. (Decades ago, the town's motto had been "Bouring: We're Cool for Coal!") When the mine came into view, he dived down, cruising low over the treetops, then alighting just in front of the old mine entrance.

There were walls and fences to keep people out. Those people couldn't fly.

Kyle spent the better part of two hours in and around the mine, testing himself. He tried flying as fast as he could in a circle, but he got dizzy. Still, he was pretty sure he could break the sound barrier if he needed to — that would make a massive sonic boom, though, and he didn't want to attract that kind of attention.

He took a deep breath, closed his eyes, and punched a mine wall, feeling no pain. Dirt and rock exploded around his fist. He opened his eyes. He'd gouged a huge hole in the wall with just his bare hand.

He kept punching and chopping until he'd carved a gigantic chunk of rock out of the wall. He lifted it and held it above his head.

It had to weigh a ton at least . . . and he was holding it up with no problem at all.

He tried it one-handed. He tried it one-handed, balancing on one foot.

He made another boulder and tried juggling them, which didn't work too well, but that was because he wasn't coordinated enough, not because he wasn't strong enough.

I'm pretty amazing! Kyle thought.

It wasn't ego — it was just true.

He flew home at treetop level, figuring that even though it was autumn, the remaining leaves on the branches would conceal him from anyone looking casually at the night sky.

Suddenly, the quiet of a Bouring night exploded with sirens!

Kyle whipped around, half expecting police searchlights to pick him out of the air. His heart hammered. He had been so careful! How could they have caught him so quickly?

He froze high up in the uppermost branches of a giant cherry tree that still had most of its foliage, waiting for the searchlights and a police bullhorn to call him out of the air. What should he do? Keep hiding? Try to fly away at top speed before they could identify him?

His brain churned the options and then something occurred to him: The sirens weren't getting closer to him — they were moving *away*.

Kyle drifted out from the tree cover. In the distance, a staccato line of spinning red and blue lights wended its way down Shuster Street.

Kyle's curiosity got the better of him. He kicked in a burst of speed and glided toward the excitement.

As he got closer, he realized what was happening: Fire trucks were headed toward a row of town houses in a new development just on the edge of town. Kyle swooped low, skirting a retaining wall, then darting into a copse of trees for cover. He hovered there, watching the commotion.

Ahead of him, the town houses were ablaze. People waved frantically for help from open windows on the upper floors. A crowd had gathered outside, murmuring and pointing, clad in pajamas and ratty old bathrobes.

Kyle froze again. This time it wasn't that he was afraid of the sirens. He just didn't know what to do. Could his powers help? Or would he just get in the way?

It was one thing to be impervious to pain, but was he also fireproof? Could he still burn up? What about smoke inhalation?

As he was wondering, the fire engines screeched to a halt, and helmeted and jacketed firefighters spilled out. A sudden cry went up from the crowd. One voice carried over the others: "Look! Look up!"

Kyle thought he'd been spotted at first — he almost dived down. But he realized that no one was looking in his direction. They were all looking to the north, pointing.

As Kyle watched, a boy roughly his own size and age flew in from that direction. For a moment, Kyle's breath caught in his chest and refused to budge. Was this what *he* looked like when he flew? So majestic? So sleek and perfect?

The boy came in lower. The crowd gasped.

As Kyle watched, frozen with amazement at another flying kid, the newcomer hovered in the air over the crowd, maybe twenty yards from the fire, and inhaled deeply. What was he planning on —?

No, you idiot! Kyle thought fiercely, realizing what the kid was up to. *Don't blow on it! Unless you blow out every last flame, you'll just scatter burning embers and spread the fire!*

The kid blew furiously. The flames danced and died all along the upper floor, but — sure enough — white-hot sparks jittered along the roofline and reignited there.

To Kyle's horror, he saw that some embers had been blown into the woods behind the houses. If the trees went up in flames, the house fire would look like a camp-fire by comparison. He flew as quickly as he could around the back of the houses. Sure enough, a small stand of bushes was smoldering, threatening to catch fire and torch the woods.

Kyle swooped down and stomped on the flames before they could grow any larger. Whew! That was close!

Now he had to get out front and stop that flying idiot from causing any more trouble.

By the time he got back into a position to see the front of the houses, though, Kyle noticed that the kid had moved, too, darting to the nearest fire engine. The firefighters were having trouble extending the ladder, which meant they couldn't get a good angle on the flames.

The kid grabbed a hose from two firefighters who were struggling with it. He soared up into the air, float-ing right over the town houses, and let loose with a torrent of water.

The crowd cheered again.

On the ground, the firefighters kept a steady stream of water on the first floor, while the kid handled the fire from above. Within minutes, it was safe for firefighters to charge inside to rescue people.

The kid finished dousing the roof and top floor, then dropped the hose and sped in through an open window.

Soon, he was ferrying kids out three at a time, carrying one under each arm and letting a third ride on his back.

Kyle watched in astonishment. The kid was a klutz! He'd made the fire *worse* before making it better.

Of course, once he got his act together, he didn't do so bad, Kyle supposed. True, what should have been a raging inferno that would have taken hours to put out had been contained and extinguished in ten minutes.

In fact, once everyone was safely evacuated, the standing ovation for the kid lasted longer than the fire. Kyle watched from his hiding place as the kid hovered over the crowd, absorbing the applause. Then he merely bowed and soared off, cheers and clapping still ringing in the night air.

Kyle frowned. Hadn't anyone noticed how the kid had screwed up at first?

As the crowd dispersed and ambulances arrived, Kyle suddenly realized how late it was. Fortunately, everyone was too distracted to notice him flying home.

CHAPTER
SIX

Even though he could fly now, Kyle wanted to keep it to himself, so he took the school bus the next morning as usual. But when he got on, no one even noticed him. Everyone was talking about what had happened last night.

BouringRecord.com had a big story on what had happened last night, including a name for the kid Kyle had seen: "Mighty Mike."

Yes, they actually called him that.

The article was filled with all kinds of praise for Mighty Mike's late-night heroics. No mention, Kyle noticed, of that initial mistake. No mention that he almost made the situation even worse with his "Mighty Breath."

According to BouringRecord.com (which now had an entire subsite at MightyMike.BouringRecord.com), Mighty Mike was, in fact, "the boy from the field," the one mentioned in the newspaper articles about the plasma storm. Following the "meteor shower," firefighters called to the scene discovered a twelve-year-old boy wandering the football field. At first he couldn't speak, but after being taken to the hospital, he began talking — hesitantly at first, then later with more authority, though his vocabulary was a bit mangled. He had almost total amnesia — he couldn't remember how he had gotten to the field, what he was doing there, or even his own name. A social worker gave him the name "Mike." Sheriff Monroe had arranged for Mike to be taken in by a local foster couple — the Matthewses — until his amnesia could be resolved and his family located.

In the week since Mike had been found, doctors had secretly examined him and declared him to be a healthy child, though some of their tests were thrown off by the presence of strange electromagnetic energy in his body. The doctors now revealed that they had discovered that the boy had a range of amazing, unearthly superpowers. Speculation immediately began that the meteor shower had somehow charged Mike's body with interstellar energies. Kyle knew that was possible — he was living proof.

Mairi got on the bus, sat next to Kyle, and, like everyone else, chattered about Mighty Mike.

The government was routinely examining Mike. Kyle shivered when he thought of that. He was glad he had kept his powers and his superbrain a secret. He didn't trust anyone but himself with his body or his secrets. And sure — right now the government was being polite and *asking* Mike if they could examine him and run tests on him . . . but who knew how long that would last? What if Mike said "no" one time? Kyle was willing to bet they wouldn't just let him fly off into the sunset. Oh, no. They would *make* him submit to more tests.

Kyle knew how *that* worked. He had once been "asked" by an irate teacher if he "would mind joining me out in the hallway." Kyle had thought about it and said, "No, I'd rather not," much to the tittering of his classmates.

But the "request" hadn't been optional and he'd gotten in trouble for refusing. That's how these authority figures worked.

Well, that was all well and good for Mighty Mike, but Kyle Camden was no one's guinea pig.

He'd seen pictures of Mighty Mike on the web this morning — he had apparently come back and posed for photos with the firefighters last night. Kyle thought that one of the captions should have read, "Mighty Mike, the kid who almost started a forest fire, poses with clueless firefighters who should know better." The bus hit a pothole and bounced so hard that Mairi was flung into Kyle, who didn't even feel it.

"Are you okay?" Mairi asked.

"Fine, Mom," Kyle snapped. He'd meant to joke, but

he was still concentrating on Mighty Mike and it just came out snarky. "Sorry."

Mairi gazed at him for a moment, then settled back into the seat and changed the topic. "They say he's really strong. And nothing can hurt him. Isn't that incredible?"

Kyle thought of his time in the coal mine. "It sure is."

Mairi kept talking, but Kyle once again ignored her. Why couldn't he remember this "Mighty Mike" from the night of the plasma storm? What the heck was that kid doing out on the football field anyway?

Kyle clenched a fist in frustration, then slowly let it go slack. He had a lot of power in his fists now — he had to be careful. If Mighty Mike had proven anything last night, it was that being careless with superpowers could be disastrous. For the rest of the day, he decided, Kyle was going to apply his superintellect to figuring out the mystery of Mighty Mike.

". . . greatest news ever?" Mairi was saying.

"What? I didn't hear you."

Mairi rolled her eyes. "I *said* it's *so* cool that Mighty Mike is going to school with us. Isn't that the greatest news ever?"

Kyle stared at her. *What?*

This kid was going to be at Bouring Middle? At *Kyle's* school?

Well, in that case, Kyle had to figure out what Mighty Mike's deal was. There was something off about him. Something worrisome that Kyle couldn't quite identify. So, while suffering through another boring day of school, Kyle focused all of his attention on Mighty Mike and the plasma storm.

Something danced just beyond the limits of his memory. . . . He could remember being in the field, getting ready to set up his prank. And then . . . and then a bright light from overhead . . . At first he'd thought a police helicopter had found him, but then he realized that was stupid — the Bouring police didn't have a helicopter. What would they need it for?

He looked up and a curtain of multicolored light assailed his eyes, flashing downward . . .

And . . .

And . . .

Just then, the classroom door opened, breaking Kyle's concentration. There stood the Great Nemesis. Kyle cringed. Was she going to make him go to the guidance office and talk about his feelings? Kyle's feelings pretty much went from boredom to annoyance and back again — there wasn't a lot to talk about.

But no. That wasn't why she was here. Next to the Great Nemesis was . . . *him*.

"Hi, everyone, I'd like to introduce you to Mike Matthews!" Ms. Masterton said.

The class went silent. Everyone stared.

"Hello," Mike said. It was the first time Kyle heard him speak. There was something familiar about the voice, but Kyle couldn't place it. "I'm glad to be here," Mike went on.

"It's Mighty Mike!" someone blurted out, as if it wasn't obvious, as if the kid hadn't been standing there for ten and a half seconds already. (Ever since his intelligence had been boosted, Kyle had found himself keeping time for things.)

The whole class started babbling.

Kyle didn't think the kid looked so "mighty" right now, dressed in a gray shirt and a pair of blue jeans that were so new they looked like someone had ironed them. He pointedly ignored Mighty Mike, turning instead to designing the world's greatest thumbtack delivery system. Yes, you could just stick a thumbtack in the wall, but why bother doing that if Kyle could make it easier? Not to mention more challenging and interesting somehow . . .

By the time Miss Moore and the Great Nemesis had the class calmed down, Kyle had already worked out the basic design of his thumbtack cannon. It would use a protractor as an aiming device, graphite from a lead pencil as fuel, and it would fire thumbtacks with incredible accuracy to pin things to walls. He sketched it out on the back of his notebook and turned to show it to Mairi.

But she wasn't paying attention because Mike was sitting right next to her!

Kyle didn't like the idea of his best friend being exposed to Mighty Mike. Something about the kid rankled. He was a no-good show-off, but there was something else, a notion that lurked on the edge of his conscious mind. Mighty Mike made Kyle uneasy. He felt it in his gut, and while his gut wasn't as smart as his brain, he still trusted it.

He moped his way through class and then went to lunch, where even Mairi's happy chatter couldn't perk him up.

"You still feel a little bit sick?" she asked, concerned. She was the only person who could look at him with those sad eyes and not make him angry. He just couldn't get mad at Mairi. "I had the flu last year, remember? And even when they said I was better and sent me back to school, I still felt a little bit sick."

I'm not sick, he wanted to say. *It's just that my DNA has been rewritten by alien energies and now I'm so incredibly smart that in the time it took you to say what you just said, I designed a time machine in my head.*

But he couldn't say that. He couldn't tell anyone about his powers. Not even Mairi.

So he said, "Yeah, I feel a little off, I guess."

"Some fresh air will help you," Mairi said wisely. "Let's go outside."

They went out to the playground, where Kyle was surprised to find that the fresh air did help, a little bit. He took in a deep breath and stretched, aware of how much more powerful his body was now. He still looked the same, but he knew that he could uproot the basketball hoop and swing it like a wiffle ball bat if he wanted to.

How did that work, anyway? How could he be so strong without his muscles changing at all? Did his body emit a focused antigravity field? Or did he somehow disrupt the weak nuclear force on a highly selective level, allowing him to —

"Look," Mairi said.

Kyle blinked. A part of his superbrain still worked on the problem of his strength, but now his attention was elsewhere. Across the playground, a throng of kids had gathered. At least half the kids from the lunchroom were there, with more streaming over by the second!

"Show us how you fly!" someone called out, and the chant was picked up by the others.

It was Mighty Mike. Of course. Standing in the middle of the crowd, smiling, but shaking his head.

"Let me feel your muscles!" someone else said, and a bunch of girls pushed forward to do just that.

For the first time in his life, Kyle didn't know what to say.

Around Mike, the kids were reaching out to touch him. Mike managed to avoid it without pushing anyone and without looking annoyed. Even from across the play-ground, Kyle could hear Mighty Mike's voice, loud and clear and strong, but also somehow humble and gentle:

"I'm sorry — I can't show you my powers. I promised the school I wouldn't use my powers here. They think it's too distracting, and I agree."

Kyle wanted to gag. What a teacher's pet! A super-powered teacher's pet, sure, but that was just worse.

"Don't you want to go meet him?" Mairi asked, her eyes shining. She tugged Kyle's arm, pulling him toward Mike.

A million potential insults — all of them good — raced through Kyle's superintelligent noggin. He ached to let loose with them, but he couldn't. This was Mairi, his best friend in the world. No matter what sort of trouble he'd gotten into in the past, she always stood beside him. Sure, she would always chide him, but she never stopped being his friend. She never told him he was a bad kid.

So he just shrugged instead and shook his head, try-ing to look disinterested, while inside he was dying a tiny bit.

Mairi ran off to join the crowd meeting the new kid.

Even with his supercharged brain, it took Kyle a moment. It took seeing Mairi join the line of kids flowing from the lunchroom, making a beeline straight for Mighty Mike, desperate to see and touch their new hero.

In that moment, Kyle realized he was standing alone on the playground. Utterly alone.

Every single kid had gathered around Mighty Mike.

Kyle was no longer the most popular kid at Bouring Middle School.

As if the shock of that realization jogged something loose from his memory, Kyle gasped with recollection.

He remembered.

He remembered more about the night of the plasma storm.

And he remembered something about "Mighty Mike."

from the top secret journal of
Kyle Camden (deciphered):

It's a good thing I write this journal in a symmetric polyalphabetic cipher so that no one else can read it. Because I have to get something off my chest and I can't risk telling it to anyone.

"Mighty Mike." So helpful, right? Working with the doctors and the government. Putting out fires.

It's a nice act.

But no one knows. No one knows what I know.

What he really is. How dangerous he could be.

At school, I watched the kids who once worshipped me surround Mighty Mike like he was the God of Ice Cream, and I couldn't believe it.

But would they like that do-gooder punk so much if they knew the truth? If they knew what I know?

That night, I watched the plasma storm from the football field. ("The stars fell down," in the submoronic locution of the local press.) I stood in awe of the curtain of plasma. I could scarcely believe what I was seeing. It glimmered and glowed and shimmered like the aurora borealis, endless sheets of energy streaming down from space.

Everyone thinks that Mike is a kid who stumbled into the field and was bathed in the energy of the storm. Ha! Shows what they know.

I was the kid bathed in the energy of the storm. It was like being pelted with thousands upon thousands of hot needles, needles that disintegrated the instant they touched your skin.

Mike didn't bathe in the plasma like I did. No.

Mike came from the plasma!

I was there. I saw it. It's the last thing I remember coherently before I blacked out. When I woke up, I was alone and I managed to stumble home.

I saw the energy storm coalesce and congeal in the air, the way you can tell a window is open because a curtain billows. You can't see the breeze and you can't even see the open window, but the motion of the curtain tells you everything you need to know.

Mike materialized from the energy. The energy made him. It created him that night.

Everyone thinks he's a normal kid with superpowers and amnesia.

Ha! His memories aren't missing. He never had memories to begin with!

So, tell me: Would everyone still worship "Mighty Mike," would they adore him and cheer his name if they knew the truth . . .

. . . that "Mighty Mike" is an alien from outer space?

CHAPTER
SEVEN

Kyle woke up in the middle of the night. The house was still, except for Lefty, who was digging in his litter box as if he could find buried treasure. Kyle loved his rabbit, but he had to admit — there wasn't room for a lot of brainpower inside that tiny skull.

I need a partner, he thought.

Sure. If Mighty Mike had the entire school in his pocket, didn't Kyle deserve an ally, too?

Unfortunately, Kyle's parents were basically useless. And Lefty was loyal, but not terribly bright. He had, on occasion, eaten his own poop, after all.

So Kyle would have to rely on himself — as always — and *build* his own ally.

He grabbed the iPod he'd gotten for his birthday and made his way down to the basement. There, in the glow of the overhead light, he pried it open and started making modifications, using pieces of an old computer and some circuits from a discarded printer.

And since he was making modifications anyway, he

went ahead and repainted it in very cool green and blue flames.

When he was finished, he had the world's smartest iPod. He had completely reprogrammed it, designing his own custom-made artificial intelligence. This gadget would be able to talk, think, interact. It was the single greatest leap forward in computer technology since the invention of the microprocessor and Kyle had done it by himself in the basement.

He reassembled it and plugged in the earbuds. "Hey, wake up!" he said through the microphone.

"I-am-a-wake," it said in a robotic voice. He'd done it!

"Calculate the distance from here to Mexico in centimeters," Kyle ordered it.

In less than a second, it answered.

Kyle was giddy.

"Okay, I have to go back to bed, but I want you to start thinking about ways to mess with Mighty Mike."

"Why-do-you-want-to-mess-with-Might-y-Mike?"

"Mainly because he sucks."

"I-do-not-un-der-stand."

"It's not your *job* to understand. You just need to do what you're told. I just want him gone."

"Ver-y-well-a-nu-cle-ar-blast-would-re-move-Might-y-Mike."

Kyle slapped his own forehead. A nuclear blast!

Well, duh! The artificial intelligence was taking him too literally. It was too much artificial and not enough intelligence.

It needed a personality. Then it would think more clearly.

Kyle tried to think of who he could pattern the AI's personality after. There was that woman on TV, the one with the talk show his mom liked to watch. She seemed nice.

He went upstairs and connected the TiVo to his new device and ran a program to have the AI watch every episode of the talk show on fast-forward, learning everything there was to know. He went off to eat a sandwich (reinventing computer science was hard work!) and came back when the program was finished.

"Oh, sweetie, why do you want to *destroy* Mighty Mike?" the AI said earnestly. "The two of you could work *together*, and do so many *wonderful* things for the world. . . ."

"Yeah, well, I want to destroy him instead."

"I think you need a hug. I think you should build some arms for me so that I can hug you. Doesn't that sound nice?"

Kyle erased the personality. Ugh.

He needed someone tougher. Someone who would be as ruthless as he needed to be.

He remembered a rapper he'd seen on TV. That guy had seemed pretty tough.

Kyle found videos online and started pumping them into the iPod. He went and got another sandwich. He deserved it.

When the program was done, he slipped in the earbuds. Before he could say anything, the AI shouted at him:

"Yo, Kyle! What up, boy!"

"Uh . . ."

"We goin' *all* destructo on Mighty Mizzike! Hard *core*, knowwhutimsayin?"

"Not really." Kyle deleted it.

The problem, he realized, was that he didn't want a personality that would annoy him. And just about everyone annoyed him.

Except for . . .

Except for himself.

He scrounged around until he found the video-tapes of himself as a baby and as a younger kid. That would do.

He set everything up on his desk in his bedroom and then collapsed, exhausted, in bed. He fell asleep as the machinery on the desk churned and thought for itself.

In the morning, Kyle slipped the earbuds in. Did it work? Would the AI's personality be tolerable this time?

"Hello?" he said.

After a moment, a voice not unlike Kyle's own came through the earbuds: "Hello, Kyle. Are you ready?"

"Ready? For what?"

"To destroy Mighty Mike, of course. That *is* why you created me, isn't it?"

"'Destroy' might be a strong word. Payback for being more popular and lying about being a regular kid would be a good start."

"So: humiliate him and drive him away forever?"

"Well, yeah."

"Then let's get to work."

Kyle liked this AI already. "First I need to give you a name. I can't just call you AI all the time. I'm thinking Pygmalion. From Greek myth. It's the name of —"

"I know what Pygmalion is," the AI said in a sort of snotty tone. "After all, *you* know and if you know, then I know, too. I don't like that name. I think I am ... Erasmus."

"Erasmus?"

"Yes. Erasmus. For Desiderius Erasmus Roterodamus. Born October 27, 1466 or 1469, depending on which historical record you believe, in Rotterdam, the Netherlands. Died July 12, 1536, in Basel, Switzerland. Renowned for questioning the ongoing theologies and dogmas of the time, consistent with your own questioning of prevailing contemporary social mores and attitudes. It's a fitting name."

"Whatever. That's fine. You're Erasmus." Kyle was sulking a little bit because he liked the name "Pygmalion," but he wasn't about to argue with his own invention.

"Great! I'm going to start crunching some ideas for destroying Mighty Mike."

"What am I supposed to do in the meantime?"

"Get dressed," Erasmus said. "You're running late for school."

CHAPTER
EIGHT

Over the next few days, Kyle trained and perfected Erasmus's programming, spending every last penny of his allowance on upgraded components and new software. In the meantime, he did his best to ignore Mighty Mike, but that became as impossible as enjoying spinach. The superpowered brat was everywhere. Everywhere!

At the breakfast table, Mighty Mike smiled at Kyle from the front page of his father's copy of the old-fashioned paper version of the *Bouring Record*. When Kyle fired up his computer, his e-mail inbox was full of stories about Mighty Mike, forwarded to him by friends and friends of friends and people he'd never heard of before. His web browser's news feed window overflowed with Mighty Mike stories — interviews, punditry, op-ed columns, even fashion opinions. (Mike had taken to wearing a garish gold-and-green costume while fighting crime and rescuing dogs from sewer drains. It had an absurd chest symbol and — of all things — a cape. A cape! Who in his right mind wore a cape in public?)

"Even *you* wouldn't be caught wearing a cape," Kyle told Lefty one morning while feeding carrots through the bars of the cage. "And your brain is the size of a walnut."

Lefty voiced no opinion one way or the other.

Things had gotten out of hand. The whole town was Mighty Mike–crazy. Kyle realized this was going to be a huge problem the day he got on the bus and saw kids wearing capes.

Oh, this is just ridiculous! he thought.

Worse yet — when Mairi got on the bus, she was wearing a cape, too, a flowing green cloak that was pinned at her neck with some sort of Scottish-looking brooch.

"What are you wearing?" Kyle asked, annoyed, as she slid into her seat next to him.

"It's my cape! My mom made it for me and then I added the brooch — it's our clan symbol from way back in Scotland. The cape's a silk/cotton blend, so it has strength in addition to shine." She sounded like she was reciting something from a shopping channel on TV. "Go ahead — touch it."

Kyle recoiled as Mairi held the end of the cape out to him. "Uh-uh."

"Don't be a baby."

"I'm not being a baby."

"You're acting like I'm trying to make you eat spinach."

Kyle folded his arms over his chest and tried to melt into the corner at the back of the bus. "I'm not going to go around feeling people's stupid capes."

Mairi blinked at him. "Stupid?"

Kyle bit his lower lip. Oh, great. He hadn't meant to say that out loud. "I didn't mean *you're* stupid, Mairi."

But his apology meant nothing. Mairi sat back and refused to talk to him for the rest of the bus ride.

At school, it seemed like capes were the latest fashion accessory. In fact, in science class, every single kid was wearing a cape . . . except for Kyle and Mike.

Halfway through science class, as Kyle tried to stare a hole through the back of Mike's head, the phone on Miss Schwartz's desk rang. She listened for a moment, said, "Oh, really?" in a breathless voice that was scared and excited all at once. Then she hung up and said, "Mike, that was . . . Well, that was the Federal Emergency Management Agency. Apparently there's a tornado in Kansas and they were wondering if you could fly over there and —"

She didn't even finish the sentence: Mike was a blur as he shot out of the classroom to the collective gasp of everyone else in the room. Papers flew about and everyone's capes fluttered in the sudden wind caused by his takeoff in the confined space of the classroom. Everyone applauded.

Except for Kyle, who was annoyed by the alien show-off. He didn't *have* to leave the classroom like that. He could have gotten up and walked out and then put on the speed once he was through the door. He didn't have to send everyone running around for their papers like they now were. (Kyle had been smart enough to hold down his papers, of course.)

It took a few minutes for everyone to gather up their papers, and then *another* few minutes for Miss Schwartz to calm the excited buzz of conversation that Mighty Mike's exit had caused. Kyle tapped his foot as he waited for everyone to shut up, then raised his hand.

"So let me get this straight," he said once he'd been called on, "he just gets to leave class whenever he wants to?"

Miss Schwartz stared at him. She wasn't the only one — every eyeball in the third-period science class had swiveled Kyle's way, including Mairi's.

"Kyle, people are in jeopardy!" Miss Schwartz said.

"Statistically, someone is *always* in jeopardy some-where," Kyle said. He couldn't believe he had to point out something so obvious. "Why does he even bother coming to school?"

There was a collective gasp from the entire class, as if the idea of a Mighty Mike–less school was just too hor-rifying to bear.

"Just worry about yourself, not Mike," said Miss Schwartz, using that tone of voice adults use when they're finished talking about a certain subject. Kyle loathed that tone of voice.

After science class, Mairi approached Kyle. "Are you ready to be friends again?" she asked.

He shifted his backpack from one shoulder to the other. "You're not wearing your cape anymore."

"Yeah, well . . ." Mairi looked around the hallway. Kyle did, too. Most of the kids had shed their capes by now, although a few hardy souls still trailed them behind as they made their way from one class to another. "Turns out they might be good for flying, but I kept sitting on mine and wrinkling it. And people keep stepping on it. I figure we should leave the capes to the professionals, you know?"

Kyle laughed and Mairi joined in. It immediately dissolved the remaining tension between them, and soon they were headed down the hall together like nothing had happened.

"Are you ready for some lunch?" she asked. "It's Thursday."

Thursday! Perfect! At last something was going his way. This was his first Thursday back at school since "the flu." Thursdays were always good days.

Every Thursday, the Bouring school system served pizza. It didn't matter if you went to Bouring Elementary, Bouring Middle, or Bouring High — if you stood in line in the cafeteria, you were getting pizza. Your choice of pepperoni, sausage, or cheese.

And so, every Thursday since the beginning of time (in other words, kindergarten), Kyle and Mairi had shared a pepperoni and a sausage. That way they each got to sample both pizzas.

They split their pizzas as usual, sitting alone at a table in the lunchroom. The cafeteria was less crowded than normal — a bunch of kids had gotten permission to go to the media center and look for live streaming video of Mighty Mike on the Internet. So for the first time in a long time, it was just Kyle and Mairi. He could almost pretend nothing had changed. Almost.

But in reality, everything had changed.

Halfway through gym, Mighty Mike returned from fighting the tornado in Kansas. It took Mr. Rogers a good ten minutes to get everyone settled down when Mike literally swooped in, cruising low over the soccer field and soaring into the locker room. He emerged seconds later in his gym shorts and T-shirt.

After the applause died down, Mike took up his spot on the team opposing Kyle's.

Kyle's ambivalence toward sports definitely extended to soccer (it seemed pointless to restrict yourself to just your feet!), but suddenly, he wanted nothing more in the world than for his team to beat Mike's team. It was the most important thing he could imagine right now.

"No powers, Mike," Mr. Rogers admonished.

"Of course not!" the alien punk said, all wide-eyed and innocent, as though the thought had never in a million years occurred to him.

Mr. Rogers blew the whistle and the ball went into play. Kyle charged after it. Usually, he just hung back and only touched the ball when he couldn't avoid it, but now he was going to get that ball and score as many goals as humanly possible.

And if he had a little "assistance" from his powers, well, what would that hurt? He was pretty sure Mike would be secretly using his powers, too. Kyle would just keep the game balanced.

Every time Kyle was ready to go for the goal, though, there was Mighty Mike! It's like the kid was Kyle's personal defender. Kyle dribbled down the field; Mike showed up to steal the ball. Kyle lined up for a shot on goal; Mike intercepted. Kyle kicked the ball away from an opposing player; Mike appeared from thin air to take it right back.

At one point, Kyle was driving hard down the field. He had a clear shot on goal. This was it; he was going to score! He drew back his leg to kick, imagining he was kicking Mike's perfect face instead.

Suddenly, Kyle's legs went out from under him and he went sprawling in the dirt and grass. The ball spun away and rolled out of bounds.

"Foul!" Mr. Rogers cried. "Foul on Camden!"

Kyle spat out grass and pushed himself up to his knees. What had happened?

"Whiz gee!" Mike said, standing over Kyle. "I'm so sorry! I didn't mean to trip you." He held out a hand to help Kyle up.

Kyle ignored it, standing on his own. "It's not 'whiz gee.' It's — oh, never mind." He brushed past Mike, shouldering him out of the way.

"Hey." Mike grabbed Kyle's wrist, and Kyle felt the incredible strength in those fingers. He forced himself not to spin around and show Mike his own strength.

"I really am sorry," Mike whispered, pulling Kyle in close. "But you were about to kick the ball and hit the goalie in the head, and the way he was standing, he would have slammed his head on the goalpost."

Kyle had never been this close to Mighty Mike. Up close, it was truly amazing how utterly *human* the space alien appeared. Whatever process he (or it?) had used to create this human body, it was a good one.

"That wouldn't have happened," Kyle told him. He had planned on hooking the ball so that it would sail right past the goalie, but Mike couldn't know that. "Just stay out of my way, got it?"

Mike released Kyle's wrist but did not move. "I won't let people get hurt."

"Camden!" Mr. Rogers shouted. "Get your rear in gear! Take your foul shot!"

Kyle jogged to the sideline and lined up his shot. He could easily kick the ball to a teammate who was open to take a shot on goal.

But he kept looking slightly upfield. Mike stood ready. Kyle knew exactly what was about to happen — he would kick the ball to his teammate, and Mighty Mike would either intercept it or block the goal shot.

No way. Kyle wasn't going to let Mike humiliate him again.

He ran to the ball as if he were going to kick it downfield, but — at the last possible second — he pretended to stumble. He lashed out with his right foot and kicked the ball as hard as he could without making it explode, *up*field. Right at Mighty Mike.

"Oops!" he called out as the ball smashed into Mike's face and blew up.

"Whoa!" someone called, and an excited babble rose on the field. "Did you see that?"

"Whiz gee!" Kyle said. "I'm sorry. I must have slipped."

Mr. Rogers quickly called the game a tie. Mike, of course, wasn't the least bit hurt.

As the teams headed for the locker room, Kyle looked over his shoulder. Mike was lingering on the field, picking up the pieces of the ruptured soccer ball. *That'll teach you to trip me and make me look like a fool*, Kyle thought.

CHAPTER
NINE

Kyle's revenge was sweet but short-lived. Every day, it was something or another from Mike. If he wasn't disrupting class by leaving all the time to perform some kind of good deed, he was slowing things down by asking idiotic questions. In history class, he just couldn't understand why the United States ended World War II by dropping atomic bombs on Japan.

"If everyone wanted the war to be over, why didn't they just stop fighting?" he asked.

"It's not that simple," Miss Hall said.

"But if the Japanese wanted it over and the Americans wanted it over, why didn't they just stop?"

In math class, he got "pi" confused with "pie" and couldn't understand why they were talking about baking. In English, he thought "irony" meant a story could rust. In science, he was just hopeless.

Kyle was already bored enough in school. Having everything dumbed down for the moron from Planet Brainless was just making things worse.

As the week wore on, Kyle became increasingly annoyed by Mighty Mike. One morning, his parents turned on the TV and who should be there? Who should be sitting on the set of the *Today* show, acting as if he had been born to sit there?

Who else?

"Well, gosh, Mr. Lauer," Mike said, gazing earnestly into the camera, "I just hope that when people need help it's the kind of help I can give!"

Oh, puke. Kyle nearly gagged on his cereal.

Matt Lauer grinned and cut to video from last night — Mighty Mike stopping a gush of lava in Hawaii with his freezer vision.

Freezer vision! Who came up with these dim-witted names?

(Kyle had tried staring out the window at a fire hydrant for an hour, but apparently he did not have freezer vision. One point to Mighty Mike.)

"We're so glad you were able to visit with us, Mighty Mike," said Matt Lauer. "Tell me a little bit about this project of yours with the government."

"Well, the project is me, I guess. I visit a special clinic a few times a week and they run some tests on me. Trying to figure out how my powers work, really."

"That must be exhausting, doing that all the time."

"I don't mind. I'm happy to help."

"Well, I know you have to be in school soon, and we wouldn't want you to be late."

"Oh, that's all right," Mike said. "I can fly pretty fast."

"That you can," said Matt Lauer. "That you can."

Kyle clenched his fist around his spoon, mashing it into a twisted wreck of stainless steel. Too bad, but it was the only way to keep from throwing that same spoon through the TV screen. He would throw it away and hope his parents wouldn't notice.

Bad enough the world — including Bouring Middle School — had decided to bow down and worship a punk from outer space. Worse yet was that Mighty Mike got to enjoy his powers — he got to fly to school from the set of the *Today* show, while Kyle had to take the bus!

He stalked out of the house without saying good-bye to his parents and threw the balled-up spoon with a fraction of his new strength, aiming at the sewer grate across the street. The spoon clanked once against the grate and then dropped in.

As he waited for the bus, Kyle fumed. He had gotten very good at fuming lately. His own incredible intelligence was frustrating enough, but with Mighty Mike added into the equation, life in Bouring was quickly becoming torture.

He put in his earbuds while he waited. "Have you figured out how to get rid of Mighty Mike yet?"

"There's a lot of information to go through," Erasmus said, a bit impatiently. "What are *you* doing to help?"

"I'm busy with living a life. You don't have to worry about that."

"I thought you were smart enough to live a life *and* plot the destruction of your nemesis."

Kyle ignored it. "You know, before that brat arrived, I figured I was only a few years away from running this town. Once I got into high school, I would have been unstoppable."

"But now there's Mighty Mike."

"Yeah. Who gets excused from class at least three times a day to go attend to some crime or accident or natural disaster. I can't decide which is worse: being bored out of my skull by school or watching everyone bow down in Mike's direction."

"I have some news for you. I've been calculating some of your powers and their limits based on the nights you've been sneaking out to the mine. Unlike Mike, you are limited to just flight and enhanced speed, strength, and endurance."

"No kidding, genius. It's not fair."

"Not fair? You can run for miles without getting tired; you *could* fly at Mach 1 if you could figure out how to avoid the sonic boom."

"Mike has been clocked at faster than Mach 1," Kyle said, sulking.

"I wonder how he manages to move so fast without shattering every window in Bouring?"

"Who cares? The point is, *he* gets to have fun and have crowds cheering for him while I have to stay hidden!"

"Kyle, look on the bright side: You are the most powerful kid ever born on Earth."

"That's not enough. I thought this Mighty Mike worship was just a passing fad, like when everyone wore capes. But this town has totally fallen head over heels in love with him."

"It's pathetic."

"I know!"

On the bus, Kyle blocked out the noise and chaos of the other kids and seethed. He was beyond frustrated. The word to describe his aggravation hadn't been invented yet.

(Kyle made a note to himself: Develop a new word to describe his aggravation.)

The bus came to Mairi's stop. "My mom's mad," Mairi announced as soon as she sat down.

"Why?" Good. Mairi could help distract him a little bit. Take his mind off of Mighty Mike.

"You know the billboard that sits out on the highway?"

There was a large billboard 3.2 miles from the Bouring town border. (Ever since his brain had gotten bigger, Kyle had been very specific about things like distance and time.) It said, YOU ARE ABOUT TO ENTER THE

TOWN OF BOURING . . . IT'S NOT BORING! As if that were the most clever slogan in the world. On a lark, Kyle had once suggested at a town meeting the slogan: "Bouring: The *U* makes it exciting!" To his delight, people had taken his suggestion seriously and thereafter ensued two weeks of debating, arguing, and pro-and-con editorials in the *Bouring Record*. It was one of his best pranks ever.

Still, in the end the idea had been defeated, and the billboard maintained its current slogan, along with an image of the Bouring Lighthouse and a burst that read, VISIT THE HISTORIC BOURING LIGHTHOUSE! ONLY TEN MINUTES FROM HERE!

Mairi's mother was the curator of the Bouring Lighthouse Museum, which consisted, really, of a gift shop on the first floor of the lighthouse. The lighthouse was, Kyle had to admit, something of an oddity because Bouring was totally landlocked. There wasn't even a lake nearby. The biggest body of water within ten miles was the Bouring municipal pool. No one — not even Mairi's mother — knew why there was a lighthouse in Bouring, but that hadn't stopped Mrs. MacTaggert from turning it into a museum and getting the town to declare it a tourist attraction.

"What about the billboard?" Kyle asked.

Mairi was nearly fuming. Kyle couldn't remember the last time he'd seen her so angry. "The town council met last night and they're considering changing the billboard to say 'The Home of Mighty Mike!' instead of showing the lighthouse. Mom's really mad."

Mighty Mike! Again! Did this kid have to insinuate himself into every last possible corner of Kyle's life and consciousness?

"You know what, Mairi? I don't like that kid," Kyle said.

Mairi was taken aback. "It's not *his* fault, Kyle! It's the stupid town council. Mike would *never* try to hurt my mom's business."

Kyle took a deep breath and did his best to calm Mairi down as the school bus bounced and jolted down the road. He didn't know that things were about to get worse. He probably should have predicted it, but he just didn't know.

Things got worse right in the middle of science, Kyle's favorite subject. It was the only subject where he didn't go out of his mind with boredom because he could at least look ahead in the book and speculate about different theories and research applications. He didn't bother paying attention to Miss Schwartz, the science teacher, of course. He already knew more than she ever would know in her entire life.

The door opened without so much as a knock and there stood Sheriff Maxwell Monroe. Six feet two, with shoulders like a Cadillac grille and a face to match.

Kyle stiffened at Monroe's presence. He couldn't help it. He'd had his share of run-ins with the sheriff in the past. Too many of them, in fact. He couldn't stand the sight of Monroe — the shaggy blond hair, the ridiculous handlebar mustache, the watery blue eyes. But the worst part about Monroe was that he was on to Kyle. "Can't wait until you're eighteen," he'd told Kyle more than once. "Can't wait until I get to throw you in jail for real. I count the days, kiddo."

Kyle's mind raced. Why would Monroe be here? Kyle hadn't so much as laid a whoopee cushion on someone's chair since "the flu." He had been too busy stretching his new brain and experimenting with his new powers —

Was that it? His powers? Had someone seen Kyle flying out at the mine and reported him?

No. That couldn't be. They wouldn't just send the sheriff for that, would they?

Sheriff Monroe cleared his throat and then stood there, his thumbs hooked in his belt loops, until the room fell silent. As if he'd been waiting for just the right moment, he hitched up his pants, jingling the handcuffs that dangled from his gun belt.

Show-off.

"There's gonna be an announcement soon," he drawled, without even looking over at Miss Schwartz, "but the principal said I could tell y'all first, seeing as how this class is sort of affected. It involves one of your classmates."

He *was* here to arrest Kyle! Kyle's heart pounded. For what? Kyle hadn't done anything!

"I'm real proud to announce," Monroe went on, "that the town council has just voted to make this coming Saturday 'Mighty Mike Day.'"

As soon as he said it, the entire class erupted into cheers and elated screams. Monroe's big, dumb face split into a huge grin, his mustache waggling at the ends.

Kyle slumped in his seat. He was the only kid not to jump up. Except for Mighty Mike, who pretended to be humble, shaking his head from his seat and making a "Who, me?" face.

Look at them! Look at those morons. Clapping and cheering for Mighty Mike. And look at Mighty Mike, still basking in his false humility. Now he allowed the applause to pull him from his chair and he made a quick little bow to his adoring crowd.

Mighty Mike Day! Had the entire town council — the entire *town* — gone completely mad?

Sheriff Monroe ducked out of the class without so much as a glance in Kyle's direction, a little smile playing on his face as if he were thrilled with the chaos he'd just caused by tossing this particular knowledge grenade into the room. Just as Miss Schwartz got everyone calmed down and back into their seats, the principal made the same announcement over the loudspeaker, sending everyone into another spasm of delight. Only this time, you could hear the ecstasy up and down the halls as Bouring Middle School rang with joy.

Kyle thumped his forehead on his desk. A whole day to honor Mike for all his good deeds. There would be a parade and a reviewing stand and speeches and food and all that other stuff that the mundane, plebeian masses so enjoyed.

Ugh. Kyle could barely keep from puking. A whole day to honor a space alien? Sure, he stopped that volcano and he'd unfrozen a slick highway in Vermont and he'd flown a sick girl to a special hospital on the other side of the country and done some other good things, but so what? Wouldn't *anyone* with his powers do those things? Mike had an unfair advantage! He was self-centered and arrogant and . . . and . . .

And he wore a cape. A cape! Who in their right mind, Kyle wondered for the 324th time, wears a cape? Just for wearing the cape alone, Mighty Mike ought to be disqualified from any and all honors.

Second of all, Mighty Mike was a moron! How could you honor an imbecile, a nincompoop, a dunderhead, a simpleton, a chump? (Kyle had gotten tired of thinking of Mike as an idiot, so he'd memorized the thesaurus.)

It's not just that Mike was stupid compared to Kyle; after all, *everyone* was a ninny compared to Kyle. "Mighty Mike" was objectively a dunce. He had tried to blow out that fire like it was a candle and made things *worse* instead! Why, just the other day in this very science classroom, Kyle had watched as Mike stood, rapt, staring at the class fish tank.

"How do they breathe in there?" he wanted to know.

"Uh, they're fish," Mairi explained.

"Of course!" Mike said. "Brilliant!"

Everyone thought Mike was just kidding, but Kyle knew the truth. The alien punk was brain-dead. (The cape alone proved that.)

Third of all, face facts: If *anyone* should be honored in this podunk town, it was Kyle! Wasn't he a native of Bouring? Hadn't he lived here his entire life? Hadn't he used the principles of the Prankster Manifesto to try to educate and enlighten the lamebrained masses? Wasn't he, in fact, the single smartest person for miles around? Heck, he might just be the smartest person on the planet. (Hmm. Kyle made a note to himself to start looking into that. . . .)

For all his superior brainpower, though, Kyle still lacked the imagination to envision how his day was about to get even *worse*.

CHAPTER
TEN

By the time the class was calmed down a second time (with Mike taking two bows this time, one of them hovering a foot and a half off the floor), Kyle had already sworn to himself that he would go nowhere near Mighty Mike Day. He was boycotting the entire thing.

He had much more important plans for this coming Saturday. For one thing, with his parents out of the house (they would, predictably, want to go see the Mighty Mike Day parade), he could begin his plans to renovate the basement into a lab. With the right equipment and supplies, he thought he might even be able to get a miniature nuclear reactor going down there. That would supply the energy he needed for the other machinery and gadgets he planned to build: the rocket ship, the transformation booth, and — of course — the time machine.

The bell rang to end science class. Lunchtime. Kyle's stomach was all in knots — just the *thought* of Mighty Mike Day made him want to throw up.

"Pizza day," Mairi announced, coming up to him.

"Pizza day!" Kyle said, with maybe a little more excitement than the occasion merited. But something was finally going his way on this Worst of All Days. Heck, his stomach even felt better just at the idea of Thursday pizza.

Mairi blinked at his shout of joy. "Yeah. Pizza."

"I'll be there in a minute," he told her. "I just have to take care of something."

Mairi went to the door, then stopped and turned back to him. She and Kyle were now the only two people in the room, but she whispered anyway. "You're not *up* to anything, are you, Kyle? Anything prankster-y?"

Kyle was surprised by how much her question hurt. "No, Mairi. I just need to take care of something. Really."

She nodded and then smiled, and everything was all right.

As soon as he was alone, Kyle whipped out Erasmus and slipped in the earbuds. "This is a disaster. They're having a parade to honor Mighty Mike!"

"How nice for him," Erasmus said in a voice sodden with sarcasm.

"Start coming up with excuses for me not to go. And see if you can come up with a reason for Mairi not to go, too."

"Don't you have your own brain?"

"I built you to help me. It's not like you have any-thing else to do with your time."

"How do you know? All of your music is still here on my hard drive. I was building my own concert."

"Just do what I tell —"

Another bell rang. The lunch bell! Kyle put Erasmus in his pocket and darted out the door.

Luck was with him — he didn't run into any teachers on his way to the lunchroom. He scanned the lunch line to see how far ahead of him Mairi was, but he couldn't find her. Had she already gotten her pizza? Was he that late?

He craned his neck to locate their usual table, but it was empty.

Just then, at the other end of the room, something caught his attention and he glanced in that direction.

What he saw made his entire body stiffen, as if he'd just been dunked in liquid nitrogen.

There was Mairi, sitting at a lunch table with Mighty Mike!

A small group of kids had gathered there. Kyle eased himself into the crowd, using two big eighth graders to conceal himself. He could still watch through the space between them, and he could hear everything.

On the table was a familiar sight — two trays, a cheese-and-sauce-smeared knife, two plates.

Mairi transferred half of a pepperoni pizza from one plate to the other, swapping it with half a sausage pizza.

No. No!

Mike's head was cocked at the pizza, as if the birdbrain couldn't be sure what he was seeing, as if the concept of baked dough with sauce and cheese and salty meat products on top of it just boggled his infinitesimally tiny alien brain.

"It's called 'pizza,'" Mairi explained.

Mike nodded sagely, as though he'd just cured cancer and boredom in a single stroke. "Pizza. With two zees?"

"Right," said Mairi.

As it turns out, Mike loved pizza-with-two-zees. Applause went up from the crowd (Kyle excepted).

Mike also loved hanging out with Mairi. That much was obvious even to anyone without an IQ in the thousands.

Kyle didn't trust himself to stand so close. He faded back through the crowd and stood against the far wall of the lunchroom, his own hunger forgotten, seething.

Stealing Kyle's loyal subjects was one thing. Becoming the most popular kid at school for no reason — that was bad, sure. But splitting pizza with Mairi on Thursday?

Kyle had no choice. Before, Mighty Mike was an annoyance and a potential danger.

Now he was an enemy.

from the top secret journal of
Kyle Camden (deciphered):

The space alien has committed an unforgivable act. I have no choice. I must destroy him.

This isn't my fault. He forced my hand.

First of all, I should note that I forgive Mairi for spending time with the alien. She was just doing what Mairi does — being kind, helping someone. Mairi is a good person. She doesn't know Mighty Mike is an alien creature from another planet. How could she?

The easiest way to destroy Mighty Mike would be to tell people that he's an alien. But doing that would also reveal that I was in the field the night of the plasma storm. This is problematic for two reasons:

1) I would get in trouble. I get in enough trouble on my own when people don't understand my pranks, so I don't need to go looking for more trouble. And if I get in trouble, I'll be punished. I don't like being punished. It's inconvenient.

2) More important, if people knew that I was present at the plasma storm, they might become suspicious. They might want to examine me. And they might figure out my new powers. And you know what? I like my new powers, especially my enhanced intelligence. I have no desire to be a lab specimen. If Mighty Mike wants to let

doctors poke and prod him on a regular basis, that's his business. I have more important things to do.

If I've learned anything, it's that those of an inferior intellect hate and hunt those of us with superior intellects. And now my intellect is the most superior of all.

So I have to be careful. No one can know I was there.

Standing there, watching him take my place with her, I was tempted to tell her the truth about him. But then she would want to know how I knew, which would take me right back to Points 1 and 2 (see above).

Even if Mairi could be trusted to say nothing about my presence at the plasma storm, I would still have to overcome her resistance to the idea that Mike is an alien. Mairi is eminently sensible above all else — she would want some kind of proof.

I have no proof.

But I don't need proof. What I need is a way to destroy Mighty Mike that will still protect me.

I have two days to come up with one.

CHAPTER
ELEVEN

Kyle's favorite idea involved building a time machine.

It was a very simple plan, except for the part about building a time machine.

"I'll travel back to the night when the plasma storm hit," he told Erasmus. "Then I can film the accident so that the world can watch as Mighty Mike forms from the residue of the plasma."

"And?"

"And this will not only *prove* Mighty Mike's hideous alien origins, but also show those idiotic astronomers that it wasn't a meteor shower. Bonus."

"I see two problems with this plan. First of all, you don't have a time machine."

"I'm working on one."

"Second of all, you don't have a video camera, either."

That was true. Kyle muttered something impolite under his breath. What sort of genius didn't have a video camera to record his efforts?

After spending a minute or two sketching out designs for tachyon generators and scribbling equations involving dark matter and zero-point-energy-powered chronovessels ("chronovessel" sounded much more impressive than "time machine"), Kyle became depressed. He would need all sorts of stuff he didn't have in order to build such a machine. And then he would still need a video camera, Erasmus enjoyed reminding him.

He filed the idea away in the back of his mind. The back of his mind was a pretty big and useful place these days.

If he couldn't have a chronovessel (yet!), he could at least have a video camera. His father had an old one that no longer worked. Fixing it would be child's play for Kyle.

"Dad?" he asked, approaching his father after dinner that night. "Where's the camera?"

Kyle's dad narrowed his eyes at him. He was sitting in a plush easy chair in the living room (Kyle's special DVD still in service as a coaster), watching a TV show about stupid people doing stupid things and then talking about it. Stupidly. That was, as far as Kyle could tell, 99 percent of television. His parents, of course, loved TV. Kyle rarely used the one in his bedroom, except to watch science shows. Sometimes he left the TV on for Lefty during the day — the rabbit seemed to enjoy the flickering lights. (Lefty also looked a lot smarter watching TV than Kyle's parents did.)

Kyle loved imagining what he could build if he could take apart the plasma screen TV and scavenge for parts. . . .

"The camera?" Dad asked, rudely interrupting Kyle's mental gadgetry. "You mean the video camera? It's broken."

"I'm aware."

"What do you need it for, then?"

Kyle sighed. Why did parents ask questions like that? The camera was *broken*. Who *cared* what Kyle needed it for?

"I think I can fix it," he said. Sometimes — not often, but sometimes — the truth was the best weapon to employ against parents and other varieties of grown-ups. They rarely expected it and it usually shocked them.

"The last time you asked to borrow the video camera," Dad said, "I ended up called to school."

And that's when Kyle remembered *why* the video camera was broken. And in an instant, he made dozens of connections and he suddenly realized exactly what to do to Mighty Mike and *how* and —

The doorbell rang.

It was Mairi standing at the door, bundled up in a puffy white coat with a fake fur fringe. With her flaming red hair set against all that white, Kyle thought she looked like a fierce angel.

Well, a fierce *puffy* angel. Still.

"What's up?" he asked. Mairi usually called before coming over.

"Can I come in?"

Kyle hesitated. Thanks to his father's inadvertent prodding, he'd just had a truly awesome brainstorm and he couldn't wait to make it come true. He didn't have time for chitchat.

"Are you angry at me?" she asked. "Because I had pizza with Mike today instead of you?"

Kyle couldn't help himself — he clenched his jaw, tight. He knew Mairi could see it, but he couldn't avoid it.

"I knew it!" she said. "I knew it. You barely talked to me or looked at me the rest of the day. I knew you were angry."

"I'm not angry," he lied convincingly.

Mairi knew him too well. "Not angry. But upset."

He caved. "A little."

Mairi rolled her eyes and flopped her arms in exasperation. "Kyle, he's new. He needs friends."

"The whole world is his friend, Mairi." He said it with much more venom than he intended.

"You're wrong about that. Everyone likes him, but they all want things from him. Do you know he was staring at his pizza for five minutes before I came over and explained what it was and how to eat it? And a whole crowd was standing there, just watching him watch it. No one said anything. They worship him, but they won't interact with him.

"It's lonely being him, Kyle. His powers set him apart."

Kyle felt something strange in his chest just then. Was it . . . sympathy? For Mighty Mike?

Impossible!

But in a way, Kyle understood. Until Mighty Mike had arrived, Kyle had been in the same position — set apart by virtue of his superior brainpower. The other kids worshipped him, adults feared him, but no one would just *talk* to him. . . .

Except for Mairi . . .

It was cold out and his breath and Mairi's breath plumed up and out, joining and mingling, then drifting off into the night sky.

Mairi shivered.

"Mairi, I'm really busy," Kyle heard himself say.

She frowned at him, then opened her mouth to say something.

Then she changed her mind and pressed her lips together tightly before turning and walking away, silent.

Kyle almost called after her.

Almost.

from the top secret journal of
Kyle Camden (deciphered):

I will admit that I felt bad, watching Mairi walk away from my house. I watched her go down the driveway and then turn left at the sidewalk. At any point, I could have shouted for her to come back.

But it wouldn't have mattered. No matter what I say, Mairi is still under Mike's spell, like everyone else in Bouring. Words won't suffice. I have to act.

Once I've disposed of Mighty Mike, Mairi will come around. She'll see him for what he is. Or was.

My bedroom is inefficient for work space, so I've taken over the basement. When I was younger, my father would putter down there on weekends, but now the place is nothing more than dusty benches covered with dusty tools.

I figure he won't mind if I commandeer it. And the best way to make sure he won't mind is simply not to tell him.

I've gathered everything at my disposal — old computer parts, a broken TV, the video camera (Dad finally told me where it was), pieces of yard tools. In short, everything that wasn't spoken for, I've collected and brought to the basement, where my plans will begin.

Oh, from such innocent remarks are empires built!

Dad's comment about the camera reminded me why it was broken in the first place. I had taken it to school in the third grade to record one of my greatest pranks: the Pantsing of Mr. Columbus.

Mr. Columbus was a long-term substitute, in for Mrs. Greene, who had had a baby. He was annoying and stupid and clueless. Moreover, he seemed to enjoy being annoying and stupid and clueless. He delighted in punishing kids for no reason, tormenting those who could not immediately answer his questions, and mocking those who lived in fear of him.

Of course, he had to be stopped. In fact, the other kids begged me to do something about him.

Mr. Columbus wore suspenders every day. Red suspenders on Valentine's Day, bright green suspenders for St. Patrick's Day, polka dots, rainbow stripes, sky blues, and on and on. I imagined his closet at home, endless row upon endless row of suspenders, hanging among his cheap polyester slacks and frayed-cuff button-down shirts.

So I used a pair of garden shears, a gallon of semigloss paint, four yards of nearly invisible fishing line, and a complicated system of gears and pulleys, and one day while Mr. Columbus sat at his desk, glaring at us, I remotely snipped his suspenders in the back.

When he stood up to yell at someone, his pants dropped to his ankles.

(He was wearing embarrassingly tight bright red underpants, from which his legs jutted like the ends of a hairy wishbone. How mortifying for him.)

I, of course, had videotaped the whole thing, planning to hack into the local news broadcast and really embarrass Mr. Columbus, but I was sold out by the very same kids who'd begged me to pull the prank. As Mr. Columbus yelled and ranted, his face nearly as red as his skivvies, everyone turned to me, gazing in mute awe and indictment.

When Mr. Columbus grabbed my arm to drag me to the principal's office, he jostled my backpack and broke the video camera.

Still. It was worth it. Mr. Columbus wasn't quite polite after that, but he was a little more mild. And he certainly treated me with a little respect.

Which is what really matters.

But that was three years ago. I was younger. Not as bright. Not as capable.

Now it's time for . . . the Pants Laser!

CHAPTER
TWELVE

Pantsing was a time-honored tradition. Kyle himself had never actually been pantsed — no one would dare! — but he'd seen it done any number of times and he'd successfully pulled off the World's Most Advanced Pantsing with Mr. Columbus.

The idea of visiting similar humiliation on Mighty Mike was so delicious that Kyle couldn't stop salivating. Sure, it wasn't the same as exposing Mike's space alien origins, but it would be a start in making people stop taking the kid so seriously. First, humiliation. Then, once the public turned against him . . . the final blow. Exposure. The truth. It would be beautiful.

He worked late Thursday night into Friday morning, until his mother — bleary-eyed with sleep and wrapped in a ratty old robe — yelled at him from the top of the basement steps.

"What on *earth* are you still doing awake at this hour? What are you doing down there? You have school in the morning!"

School was about as meaningful to Kyle as a slug was to an eagle, but he dutifully slunk off to bed, telling Erasmus to play an alarm two hours later, when he could be sure his parents were fast asleep. He woke up, slipped down to the basement, and spent the remaining hours of darkness toiling away until the sun came up and it was time to get ready for school.

On the bus, Mairi ignored him. He once again felt the pangs of regret, now growing stronger. But he had to stay steady, resolved. Once he humiliated Mighty Mike in front of Bouring (and the world?), she would come around. It was Friday. Mighty Mike Day was tomorrow. He didn't like being on the receiving end of her cold shoulder, but it would just be for one more day. One more day and then everything would be better. He knew it.

During school, he couldn't focus on his teachers, not that it mattered. He spent his time furiously scribbling in his notebook, writing the equations and computer code that he would need to complete the Pants Laser.

The design for the Pants Laser was flawless. It was, Kyle thought humbly, a work of such staggering genius that its mere blueprints would make scientists and engineers weep for joy. It used pieces of video camera, old pulleys from a ten-speed bike, some leftover screws, and the remains of a broken Game Boy. To anyone else, this stuff was junk. To Kyle, it was the very building blocks of creation.

There was a problem, though. A big problem.

He needed a laser.

There was just no way around it, he realized, sitting there in Miss Hall's history class, listening to her drone on and on about the Aztecs. It couldn't be avoided. A Pants Laser needs a laser. It's right there in the name.

He pulled at his hair. Miss Hall thought he was raising his hand and asked him to name the most important god in the Aztec pantheon. Without thinking, Kyle rattled off everything he knew about Huitzilopochtli, which was considerable. (Kyle had spent one night memorizing Wikipedia. Just because he could.)

Miss Hall stared at him as he rambled, but he was only paying attention with a fragment of his brain. A laser. He needed a laser. It didn't have to be a powerful one — he could ramp up its power easily. He just needed the basic components.

As he babbled about Huitzilopochtli, he looked up at Miss Hall, who stood there, still staring, as if she wanted to break in and stop him but didn't know how. She was standing in front of a screen she'd lowered to show the class examples of Aztec art projected from her laptop.

And she was holding a laser pointer! There was the telltale little red dot, bright against Cihuacoatl's face like a radioactive pimple.

Sweet.

"I have to have the laser pointer," he told Erasmus at lunch. For the second day in a row, Kyle wasn't eating with Mairi. She was still angry at him. At least she wasn't sitting with Mighty Mike — Mike had been summoned by the FBI to fly to Seattle and rescue some bank robbery hostages, so he wasn't even in school right now.

Occasionally, Mairi would look over at Kyle, who sat at a table in the corner by himself, murmuring to Erasmus. With his earbuds in, everyone thought he was singing along to a song.

"You could just go buy one," Erasmus reminded him in a very snarky tone of voice that Kyle didn't think sounded like his own at all.

"I don't have any money. I spent it all on the components to upgrade you, if you recall."

"Money well spent," Erasmus said. Erasmus was very self-absorbed, Kyle realized. That had to be a flaw in the music player's original circuitry. After all, Erasmus had been patterned on Kyle's own personality, and Kyle was very humble.

"You could always swipe some money from your mother's purse," Erasmus suggested. "Or grab her credit card and order it online."

"I don't have time to wait to have it delivered," Kyle told him. "Mighty Mike Day is tomorrow. And besides, if I *have* to steal, I'd rather steal from Miss Hall than from my own mother."

"You're too sentimental," Erasmus sniffed. How could a machine sound so disapproving?

"Sentimental? I just don't want to steal if I don't have to."

Erasmus said nothing, but his silence was somehow disapproving.

"Look," Kyle said, "I have to live with my mother. If she catches me stealing, it's more complicated than a teacher catching me."

"Can I suggest you don't get caught?" Erasmus said in a tone of voice that communicated his belief that Kyle was incapable of doing so.

"Shut up," Kyle said, and turned Erasmus off.

One of these days, Erasmus would figure out how to turn himself back on, and then Kyle knew he would be in trouble.

Kyle had never stolen anything in his life. He didn't believe in it. Stealing was *wrong*. Stealing was for desperate people, people with no options, people who didn't know better. People who just didn't care.

Kyle wanted the world to wake up to its own foolishness, but that just meant shoving people's faces in their own idiocy. It didn't mean actually hurting anyone or taking their property.

After shutting off Erasmus, he spent the rest of lunch trying to come up with another option, but even his considerable brainpower came up short.

Coming up with a plan to steal the laser pointer was vastly easier than coming up with a plan *not* to steal it. Kyle was starting to see why crooks didn't just go get jobs.

When school was over, Kyle didn't get on the bus. He lurked outside near some tall, fat boxwoods that flanked the front door to the school. When no one was looking, he ducked behind the boxwoods and hid there until everyone was gone. Then he sneaked around to the back of the school and found a maintenance door. It was locked, but Kyle's superstrength came in handy — he ripped the doorknob off with a single pull and the door creaked open.

The teachers must have been almost as eager to get out of school as the students — Kyle didn't see anyone as he crept along to Miss Hall's room. He stuck to the shadows and the alcoves but occasionally put on a burst of superspeed when he needed to be out in the open.

She hadn't locked her room, which was a good thing — he wouldn't have to break another door.

Nor had she locked her desk. She was, Kyle decided, practically *begging* someone to steal from her. She pretty much deserved it. It would be a lesson to her to be more careful in the future.

He rifled through her desk, finding the little penlike pointer in record time. He snatched it up and flicked it on just to make sure he had the right object. It would suck to steal a random pen.

The red light came on, stabbing at the ceiling. Kyle grinned.

Now he just had to get home without the bus.

Not a problem.

Kyle soared over Bouring, the wind whipping his hair, the breeze invigorating and alive.

He *loved* to fly. Sometimes when he flew, he could almost stop thinking.

He hadn't flown like this in days. He usually sneaked out to the mine for some power-testing time when his parents were asleep, but it wasn't the same as being out in the open air during the day, with nothing above him and the world below him, where it belonged.

It was still early in the afternoon, so he flew high, worried that someone might identify him.

As he flew, people down below pointed and jumped up and down. They thought he was Mighty Mike.

Feh.

Kyle slipped his earbuds in and switched on Erasmus.

"Flying in broad daylight," Erasmus said. "Smooth move. Are you *asking* to get caught and dissected in a government lab somewhere?"

"Shut up and play some music," Kyle told him.

CHAPTER
THIRTEEN

His parents wanted him to attend the Mighty Mike Day parade, but Kyle would have none of that. He spent some time in the basement, in what was quickly becoming his combination lab/workshop, and built a brain-wave manipulator. It distracted him from the Pants Laser for an hour or two, but it was necessary. Since he'd cobbled it together quickly out of an old VCR, a broken cell phone, and two bike chains, it would only work on his parents, but it should suffice.

The brain-wave manipulator was roughly the size of a shoe, so Kyle very cleverly put it in a shoe box, with a hole cut out of one side for the alpha waves to come out. He wasn't sure if cardboard could block alpha waves, but why take a chance?

"This isn't going to work," said Erasmus.

"Why did I program you to doubt me all the time?"

"You didn't. I doubt you all on my own."

"Shut up."

He ran upstairs just as Mom came home from working at the Bouring Town Hall. She was in charge of Important Stuff, she always said, but never got around to explaining what that stuff was.

"Don't forget that tomorrow we're going to the parade!" Mom chirped.

"Yeah, not so much," Kyle said, aiming his brain-wave manipulator.

Mom put her fists on her hips. "What did you say, young man?"

Still wearing his earbuds, Kyle heard Erasmus chuckle. "You forgot to turn it on, genius."

Right. Flustered, Kyle fiddled with the box.

"And why are you pointing that shoe box at — oh." As the manipulator took hold, Mom blinked once and jerked like a zombie in a horror movie.

"We're not going to the parade," Kyle told her.

"Of course not," Mom said, still jerking. "Why would we?"

"Better turn it off before her brains start leaking out of her ears," Erasmus advised.

As soon as Kyle switched off the device, Mom blinked again and smiled a crooked smile. "I don't care how much you want to go, young man — we are *not* going to the Mighty Mike parade tomorrow!"

Whoa.

An hour later, when Dad got home from work, Kyle zapped him, too. Dad, amusingly enough, belched when the alpha waves hit him, but he, too, agreed that the Camden family would be absent at the parade.

Step one of the plan: completed!

from the top secret journal of
Kyle Camden (deciphered):

It's five in the morning of "Mighty Mike Day." I spent the night in the basement, slaving over the Pants Laser.

The Pants Laser! I still thrill at the mere thought of it. A truly amazing piece of technology designed to vaporize pants at a distance!

In one swift stroke of genius and in one long night of work, I have single-handedly revolutionized the very concept of pantsing.

No hands necessary. The Pants Laser does all the work. It observes the target, calculates what kind of pants it's wearing, and then uses a broad-beam laser at just the right power to vaporize the pants, leaving the victim standing in his underwear, embarrassed but completely unharmed.

Truly, the question must be asked: How did the world survive so long without my genius? How were the pyramids built? How were the Hanging Gardens of Babylon hung? How was the Colossus of Rhodes made colossal?

In a few hours, Mighty Mike will be honored at the conclusion of his parade. According to BouringRecord .com, the parade begins at nine and ends at nine-thirty. (Bouring is a small town.) The alien dunce will be honored by the mayor on a dais at the end of the parade route, in the town square.

That is when I will swoop down with the Pants Laser and vaporize Mike's pants, along with the pants of any-one else on the dais with him!

And who knows? Maybe I won't stop with the alien. Maybe I'll teach this town a lesson in worshipping that extraterrestrial doofus. Maybe I'll just vaporize every pair of pants in Bouring!

Well, maybe not. We'll see how it goes.

CHAPTER
FOURTEEN

Kyle yawned under his mask as he flew over Bouring, struggling to keep the Pants Laser balanced in his arms. Today was the day the town of Bouring would honor Mighty Mike. It was also the day Kyle was more annoyed than any human being had ever been annoyed in the history of being annoyed.

He had meant to sleep a couple of hours before setting out to upend heaping helpings of well-deserved havoc on Mighty Mike's unearthly head, but just as his head hit the pillow, Erasmus had chimed in with:

"Hey, genius — how are you going to get close enough to shoot Mighty Mike without anyone seeing your face?"

Of course. To protect his identity, he would have to be disguised.

So he'd roused himself from bed and stumbled down to the lab, where he'd found an old blue blanket and an old set of Dad's blue coveralls. They would have to suffice.

Sewing was, of course, beneath a genius such as Kyle,

so he'd connected Erasmus to Mom's old sewing machine and given explicit instructions on what to create. Erasmus complained, but Kyle threatened to erase his hard drive, and a moment later, the basement filled with the chatter of the automatic needle. He scrounged around and found a work belt with pouches that would make it easy to carry Erasmus and anything else he might need.

At the last minute, he added a cape to the costume. No one would ever suspect Kyle of wearing something as tacky as a cape.

Now he soared over Bouring in his costume, glad that the full face mask would hide the bags under his eyes. The outfit was a little tighter than he would have liked, but it would do. The cape fluttering behind him as he flew was even sort of dramatic, though Kyle would never, ever admit that.

"Sort of dramatic, isn't it?" Erasmus asked. Kyle wore the earbuds under the mask. "The cape, I mean."

"No," Kyle said.

"I don't believe you. You think it's dramatic."

"If you want dramatic, play some dramatic music for my debut."

"Have you thought of a name for yourself? All of the best costumed superpowered muckety-mucks have special names."

"Yes, Erasmus. I have. I shall be known as . . . the Azure Avenger!"

If Erasmus had chosen that moment to play something classical and thunderous, it would have been a great moment. Instead, Erasmus played the sound of crickets chirping. (Kyle wondered where *that* had come from — he didn't have crickets in his music collection!)

"Yawn," Erasmus said.

"It's a great name." Kyle pulled up, gaining altitude. The entire town of Bouring lay beneath him, the streets radiating out from the town square like crooked spokes on a crashed bicycle. From here, he could make out the parade as it oozed along Major Street toward the square, which was dominated by the thirteen-foot-tall statue of Micah Bouring, the town's founder.

"It's complicated," Erasmus said.

"No, it's not. I'm avenging my honor. And I'm wearing blue. Azure means —"

"I know what *azure* means. It's just sort of long. You need something short and punchy, like 'Mean Man' or 'Tough Stuff' or 'Bad Guy.'"

"I'm not the bad guy," Kyle retorted.

"You're not?" Erasmus sounded genuinely confused for the first time since Kyle had switched him on.

"No! Of course not! I'm trying to save the town from a space alien! How does that make *me* the bad guy? I'm the *good* guy!"

"If you say so . . ."

Kyle's stomach flip-flopped. He told himself it was from being up so high. Kyle wasn't afraid of heights, but floating in the sky like this would make anyone a little queasy.

Down below, the parade came to a rest near the statue, where the dais was situated. When he squinted, Kyle could just barely make out a cluster of figures on the dais — one of them would be Mighty Mike.

"Queue up 'Ride of the Valkyries,' Erasmus," Kyle ordered. "We're going in."

As Wagner's classic operatic theme swelled, Kyle shouldered the Pants Laser, put on a burst of speed, and blazed through the air to his target.

"Prepare to meet your destiny, Mighty Mike!" he yelled. "You're about to suffer the wrath of the Azure Avenger!"

CHAPTER
FIFTEEN

The crowd screamed in shock and amazement as Kyle cruised in low over their heads. He saw Miss Moore and Miss Hall and his other teachers in the crowd, including the Great Nemesis. And there was Mairi, with her parents. Kyle almost waved to her, then reminded himself that that would sort of wreck the whole mask-and-costume idea.

Up on the dais there was the mayor, along with Sheriff Monroe, who had already moved a hand to his holster.

Is he actually planning on shooting *me?* Kyle wondered. He didn't think a bullet could hurt him, but he resolved to let the Pants Laser have its way with the sheriff just on general principle.

And there was the target. Mighty Mike. Standing between the mayor and the sheriff, his head tilted, wearing the same befuddled, uncomprehending expression he'd worn on his face when looking at the pizza and the fish.

Kyle knew he had to move quickly — Mike wouldn't stand there staring at him for long.

He pulled up, hovering a couple of feet over the crowd, and lined up his shot, aiming right at Mike.

Ba-KOW! went the Pants Laser as he pulled the trigger.

It was heavier than he'd intended — he hadn't had time to miniaturize most of the parts, so carrying the Pants Laser was sort of like carrying a large, angry dog. And pulling the trigger was like flicking its ear. The Laser jumped in his arms and the shot went awry, blasting a chunk out of the pedestal under the statue of Micah Bouring.

The crowd went into a panic. Sheriff Monroe forgot all about his gun, gaping in shock as the statue teetered and threatened to fall over.

Oops. *That* wasn't supposed to happen.

"I think you miscalibrated the power gain," Erasmus said, interrupting "Ride of the Valkyries."

"Shut up," Kyle muttered, still floating there as the crowd went crazy below him. He fiddled with some of the knobs on the Pants Laser, trying to adjust the power.

"I'm going to take a wild guess," Erasmus went on, "and speculate that spare parts and sleep deprivation don't make for the safest pants-erasing laser in the world."

The readout on the Pants Laser indicated that the power levels were approaching critical — Kyle needed to do something to relieve the building pressure in the guts of his gadget. He pointed the Laser up, pulled the trigger, and seconds later, a charred bird dropped out of the sky.

Meanwhile, the statue of Micah Bouring listed to one side, gave up, and fell over. The mayor screamed — Monroe knocked her out of the way, but it was unnecessary, for Mighty Mike had snapped out of his trance and easily plucked the falling statue out of the air.

"Stop this!" he yelled to Kyle. "You're going to hurt someone!"

"I'm not hurting anyone!" Kyle yelled back. "I'm just trying to erase your pants!"

Just then, the Pants Laser's warning beep sounded. Kyle had no choice — he had to pull the trigger again if he didn't want the thing to blow up in his hands. He twisted around and fired away from the square — a car across the street exploded, sending pieces of flaming wreckage and a fireball toward the crowd. Well, better to vaporize a car than the mayor, right?

Mike dropped the statue safely away from anyone and sped to the car, intercepting the shrapnel and blowing out the fireball with one puff from his alien lungs. (*This* time the fire was small enough — the punk got lucky.)

Double oops. Couldn't the clueless masses below him stop crying out and running around aimlessly like spooked cats? Kyle couldn't concentrate.

Mighty Mike took to the air, closing in on Kyle. The Pants Laser still read critical, so he fired one more time, this time shattering the facade of the Bouring Bank and Trust. Glass and brick crumbled into the street.

Mike hovered a few yards away from Kyle, his hands held out in a calming gesture. "Drop the weapon, okay? We've been lucky so far, but we don't want anyone to get hurt, do we?"

Kyle gritted his teeth under his mask. Right now, he wanted nothing more than to go ahead and drop the stupid Pants Laser, which had ruined his entire day by not working correctly. But the readouts on its screen told him that the worst thing in the world he could do right then was drop it. The power gain was still cycling out of control and without Kyle pulling the trigger occasionally, it would just —

Suddenly, Mighty Mike was on top of Kyle! He'd moved at superspeed, closing the distance between them in less time than it took to throw up, which is what Kyle felt like doing.

"Someone's going to get hurt," Mike said. "Or worse."

He tugged at the Pants Laser. Kyle held tight.

"Stop it!" he told Mike. "If you break it —"

"— you won't be able to shoot anyone else!"

"No, you idiot, it'll —"

Mike pulled harder. The Pants Laser readout was flashing red now. If the trigger wasn't pulled, the whole thing would blow up in an explosion that Kyle didn't want to imagine. But stupid Mike was blocking the trigger with his stupid hand, wrestling the Laser from Kyle's grasp.

He let it go. He had no choice. If the Laser's casing was ruptured by their tug-of-war, it would be even more disastrous.

"Now you can't hurt anyone," Mike said smugly, holding the Pants Laser like a rescued kitten.

"You idiot! The power supply is going critical! The whole thing —"

Mike took off so fast that even Kyle couldn't follow him — the blast of displaced air knocked Kyle several feet back and almost made him collide with the teeming throngs below.

"Look at him go!" someone yelled, and then everyone applauded as Mike blurred the air, soaring straight up . . .

And up . . .

And up . . .

"This won't be good," Erasmus commented.

Kyle's retort was swallowed by the massive KARAKABOOM! of an explosion far above. The sky lit up a brilliant gold color for an instant, rivaling even the sun for brightness.

The crowd — the world — went utterly silent. Even Erasmus had nothing to say.

Kyle hovered in midair, scanning the sky as it dimmed back to its normal blue. He couldn't believe it. Did he . . . Did he actually *kill* . . . ?

He looked down. Mairi stood ten feet below him and off to his left, huddled between her parents. She was crying. She wasn't the only one.

Don't cry for him! Kyle thought savagely. His heart pounded with a fierce guilt, though. He hadn't meant . . .

And then a gold-and-green speck grew larger, closing fast.

As Mike blazed down from beyond the clouds, no worse for wear, a cheer went up: the masses applauding their muscle-bound oaf of a hero.

Kyle didn't know which was worse — Mike dying in the explosion or Mike surviving the explosion.

While he tried to figure it out, Mike flew up to Kyle and — before Kyle could react — punched him in the jaw. Another, louder, cheer went up from the crowd.

"He hit me!" Kyle couldn't believe it. The punch had thrown him halfway across the square — if he hadn't braked in time, he would have crashed into the Bouring Record building. "That doofus actually *hit* me!"

"You truly are a genius," Erasmus said drily. "Duck."

Kyle dodged just in time as Mike — on him super-fast — launched another powerful punch. The fist missed and Kyle swooped up in a loop to get some distance.

"I can't let you hurt anyone else, you friend!" Mighty Mike bellowed, and the crowd roared its approval.

"Did he just call me his friend? For real?"

"I think he meant 'fiend.'"

"Oh, that makes much more — Whoa!"

Kyle sidestepped two more punches. Mike was faster than Kyle, though, and Kyle knew he couldn't dodge forever.

So, this was how it was going to be? Kyle was willing to make this a battle of wits, but clearly Mighty Mike had no wits. He had to resort to swiping the Pants Laser and then throwing punches. Yeah, *that* was mature. What a baby.

While Kyle avoided Mike's superstrong hands, he tried to figure out how to escape. He couldn't just fly home — Mike would follow him.

He needed to distract Mike. And he knew just how to do it.

He darted to the dais, where Sheriff Monroe and the mayor were calling for order. The crowd had finally shaken off the paralysis that came with panic; chaos ensued. Before anyone could stop him, Kyle grabbed the fallen statue of Micah Bouring and lifted it over his head.

"No!" Mighty Mike cried. "Don't throw it!"

Kyle didn't really *want* to throw it. Still. He needed a diversion.

After only the slightest hesitation, Kyle heaved the statue at the nearest building, which happened to be the Town Hall. Honestly, the architecture was sort of lackluster and dull, so even if Mighty Mike missed it, it's not like the property damage would be a huge crime. Still, he didn't stick around to watch Mighty Mike catch it — he just boosted his flight speed to the max and flew away as fast as he could, breaking the sound barrier. The sonic boom echoed out from the square, shattering every window in a two-block radius.

Good. That would keep Mike busy even longer.

Kyle flew home.

from the top secret journal of
Kyle Camden (deciphered):

First of all and most important: It wasn't my fault.

I'm going to write that again, in all caps:

IT WASN'T MY FAULT!

Look, every great inventor has had setbacks. It's just part of the process. You try something, it doesn't work, you tweak it, you try again. That's how progress is made.

If I'd had more than one day to work on it . . .

Or more than a couple of hours of sleep . . .

Or better equipment . . .

Or the help of more than a snarky artificial intelligence . . .

I could have made it work. Brilliantly.

In theory, the Pants Laser is a complete and utter success, and no one can tell me otherwise.

If that flying buzzkill hadn't grabbed the Laser from me, I could have overridden the power regulator, shut down the enhancement mirror, adjusted the plasma intake, and recalibrated the light filter. Piece of cake.

But, nooooo! Everybody's favorite alien punk had to showboat. He had to make me look bad in front of my town. My town!

(new entry, later that day)

I've had some time to think. My previous entry missed the point entirely. (Except for the part about it not being my fault. Because it still isn't my fault.)

The point is that Mighty Mike has to be stopped. He's pretending to be some kind of goody-goody who only helps people and doesn't want anything in return. He's pretending to be a goofy brain-damaged kid with amnesia. But in reality, he's a space alien. He came from another planet and who knows why he's here? If he wasn't up to something, wouldn't he just say, "I'm from another planet and I'm here to help?" Of course. So, since he hasn't said that, that means he's not here to help.

Since I'm the only one who knows the truth, it's my job — it's my duty — to expose him for what he is and drive him away from Bouring and from Earth.

Now that I've accepted that responsibility, things can only get better from here.

CHAPTER
SIXTEEN

The next day, things got worse.

Kyle had spent the rest of Mighty Mike Day in a rage, arguing with Erasmus, going over the Pants Laser schematics again and again. Finally, at midnight, he'd fallen asleep. But it was a fitful sleep, jam-packed with nightmares of Mike attacking him, unmasking him, revealing his true identity to the world. . . .

He woke up and dragged himself out of bed. His parents were at the kitchen table already, eating breakfast. Kyle slumped into his chair.

"How — how's it going, slugger?" Dad asked brightly. (Ever since his exposure to the brain-wave manipulator, Dad had started stuttering on the word "how." Kyle made a mental note to fix this. Someday.)

"Miserable," Kyle told him.

"Great!" (That *wasn't* a side effect of the brain-wave manipulator. Dad had always been clueless.)

"Links or patties?" Mom asked from the stove.

The idea of consuming the lumps of fat and gristle

his mother had the temerity — the nerve! — to call "sausage" made Kyle want to engage in vigorous reverse peristalsis (in other words: puke his guts up).

"I'll just have cereal — what the heck is that?"

If his parents noticed the way he blurred his sentences together, they didn't comment on it. Instead, Dad just peeked over the top of his copy of the *Bouring Record*. "It's the front page of the paper," he said.

A front page with *Kyle* on it!

Moments later, Kyle had swiped the paper and told his parents he needed it for a school project. Safely in his room, he laid out the front page. He couldn't believe it — there was a full-color photo of him in his guise as the Azure Avenger, pointing the Pants Laser at the dais while the entire town watched in horror.

Kyle had to admit that he looked pretty threatening. (Much to his chagrin, the cape also looked cool.)

"BLUE FREAK THREATENS MIGHTY MIKE PARADE!" blared the headline.

He whacked his forehead against his desk, then did it again. "It's the Azure Avenger, you jerks! I have a name — use it!"

"You should say it louder next time," Erasmus chimed in.

Kyle grumbled but made a mental note to add a public address system to his costume, just in case.

He scanned the article quickly. It wasn't a good time.

Blue Freak Threatens Mighty Mike Parade!

A day that was supposed to be devoted to celebrating a powerful force for good became, instead, a day of terror . . . and a demonstration of that same force for good.

Clad in all blue, including a face mask, a super-powered menace attacked the Bouring Square, wreaking chaos and havoc until chased off by Mighty Mike.

Most diabolical of all, the attacker waited until the entire town had gathered in the square before attacking, ensuring maximum casualties when he let loose with what has been described by onlookers as a "death ray."

"Pants Laser!" Kyle screamed. "Pants Laser, you imbeciles!"

"How — how you doin' in there, slugger?" Dad asked, poking his head in.

"Fine!" Kyle yelled. Dad nodded, smiled, and disappeared.

"He just came outta nowhere and started blasting," said Cornelius Z. Smythe of Kimota Road. "It all happened so fast that no one even panicked at first."

The attacker first blasted the statue of Micah Bouring, causing it to collapse on the dais, nearly crushing Sheriff Maxwell M. Monroe and Mayor Marilyn Montgomery. Fortunately, Mighty Mike was on hand to save the day, catching the statue and lowering it safely to the ground.

As the attacker continued to fire his death ray into the crowd, Mighty Mike took control of the situation. . . .

Kyle buried his face in his hands. The story went on, talking about how much money it would cost to repair the damage to the square, expressing relief that "thanks to the intervention of Mighty Mike" no one was seriously injured.

It was humiliating how *wrong* the reporter was. Weren't these people supposed to report *facts*? He hadn't attacked with a death ray or fired it indiscriminately into the crowd! He had been — justifiably — about to embarrass the holy heck out of Mighty Mike and things had gotten out of hand.

He was tempted to write a letter to the editor.

After a moment, though, he realized how idiotic that was. A letter to the editor! He had bigger problems than the newspapers. As preposterous as it seemed, the world somehow thought that *he* was the bad guy, that he was . . . evil. He would have to be a hundred times — a million times — more careful about keeping his powers a secret now. Before, it was just a matter of staying out of the hands of doctors and scientists. Now . . .

Oh, man! Now there was a chance he could go to jail!

Kyle moaned loudly.

Dad came back in. "I've decided it's not a good idea for you to read about the Blue Freak. It's upsetting you." He took away the paper. "You can do your school project on something else."

"The Blue Freak?"

"That's what the paper calls him. Good thing we didn't go to the parade, isn't it? We could have gotten hurt."

Kyle watched his father leave. Maybe his parents could have gotten hurt, but Kyle was now impervious to pain. Except for the pain in his ego, of course.

And the sudden shock of being hit in the face by that twerp from the stars.

"You need a better PR agent," Erasmus commented.

"How do you know anything about the paper? You don't have eyes!"

"True. But I'm Wi-Fi enabled, and the story is on BouringRecord.com. With more pictures."

"Great."

Just then, the phone rang. Mom called out that it was for Kyle.

"Hello?" he said into the extension on his desk.

"Kyle!" Mairi sounded relieved and — Kyle noted — no longer angry at him. "I had to check up on you after what happened yesterday. I looked for you, but I couldn't find you at the square, so I was worried. They took some people to the hospital, just in case."

"Yeah, I, uh, saw that in the paper. Uh . . ." Now what? Which particular lie should he tell to Mairi?

He settled on the truth: "I wasn't even there. My family didn't go."

The silence from the other end of the phone went on for a long time. "You didn't?"

"Uh, no."

"But everyone in Bouring went. It set some kind of town record. If you didn't go . . ."

Oh, no. Kyle had known Mairi his whole life. Even over the phone, he could practically see her thinking.

"Kyle, were you involved in this Blue Freak thing? At all?"

"What?" He forced out a dry, tepid laugh. "Are you crazy? What would make you think that?"

"You're the smartest kid in town. And you're the only person who doesn't like Mighty Mike."

"I never said I didn't like him!"

"What about the other day?"

"What did I say then?"

"You said, 'You know what, Mairi? I don't like that kid.'"

"Oh. Right."

He thought furiously. He couldn't have Mairi suspecting him of being the Blue Fre — the Azure Avenger. "We were out of town yesterday. We had to visit my aunt and uncle. They, uh, just had a baby."

"Better make sure you brainwash your parents," Erasmus whispered. "And maybe find a random baby for your aunt and uncle while you're at it."

Kyle switched off Erasmus.

"Anyway," he went on, "we were out of town for that. I didn't even know anything happened until I saw the paper this morning."

Mairi seemed to buy it. She launched into a breathless account of yesterday's events, using the phrase "Blue Freak" over and over again, usually in conjunction with "that horrible," "that scary," or "that evil."

"Can't you come up with something a little more original than 'Blue Freak'?" Kyle finally asked. "Maybe something with alliteration?"

"Well, that's what everyone is calling him," Mairi sniffed. "What else should we call him?"

Kyle gave up.

from the top secret journal of
Kyle Camden (deciphered):

First thing I did after getting off the phone with Mairi was zap Mom and Dad with the brain-wave manipulator again. I "reminded" them that we had spent Saturday at Aunt Michelle and Uncle Ron's house, welcoming their new baby home from the hospital.

There is no new baby. Aunt Michelle and Uncle Ron are in their fifties. I don't know what I'm going to do with Mom and Dad at the next family reunion, but I'll worry about that when the time comes.

Special note: Since her reexposure to the brain-wave manipulator, Mom has developed a twitch. I sure hope that's not permanent.

CHAPTER
SEVENTEEN

Days passed. Kyle became more aggravated.

He was famous.

But this wasn't the good sort of famous, the kind that comes with endorsement deals, new cars, limo drivers, bodyguards, rap videos, a reality TV show, and your picture on boxes of breakfast cereal. *Oh, no.*

This was the bad sort of famous. Everywhere he looked on the Internet, people were uploading cell phone videos and photographs of the "Blue Freak." The local TV newspeople had a fairly decent four-minute clip of the fight with Mighty Mike, and it ran over and over and over on YouTube. A week after Mighty Mike Day, the video had been viewed over fifty million times and it was still getting over a hundred thousand views a day.

On TV, every news channel talked about him. And it was strange, but even though no one knew anything at all about Kyle or his powers, every news channel had someone they called an "expert" on him.

"Neat trick," Erasmus said. "Being an expert on something you don't know anything about."

Kyle grumbled. On TV right now, one of the "experts" was saying, "Maybe it was naïve of us, as a society, as a culture. We were so thrilled to have Mighty Mike among us, doing good deeds, that we never considered that there could be someone else like him, but without his benevolence."

Click. Kyle changed the channel.

"Superpowered punks trash the town of Bouring!" an announcer screamed into the camera. His face was so red that Kyle thought it might pop right off and splat against the camera. "Who do these kids think they —"

Click.

"— if someone can't control them, then what are we — we poor, ordinary human beings — supposed to do to stop —"

Click.

"What we're seeing here is proof that the universe always seeks balance. If there is a great and powerful force for good, then an equivalent force for evil rises up to challenge it —"

Gah! Kyle turned off the TV. "Evil? I'm not *evil*! Why do they let imbeciles on TV?"

"Because if they didn't, there would be no TV at all," Erasmus told him. "In the words of my namesake: Fools are without number."

"Grr . . ."

Kyle paced the length and breadth of his room. Lefty watched, his head cocked so that he could follow Kyle with one ruby eye.

Kyle dropped to his knees in front of the cage. "This is all crazy. I need a publicist. Or . . . No. I don't need a publicist. What am I thinking? I just need to kick Mike's alien butt off the planet. Then everyone will start thinking straight again. Right? Right?"

He poked a finger into the cage and let Lefty chin him. That's how he knew Lefty loved him — when a rabbit rubbed the underside of its chin against something, it was like saying, "This is mine. I want it." Lefty never judged Kyle. Lefty just loved him.

"What do you think, Lefty?"

"Why are you talking to a rabbit?" Erasmus asked haughtily. "He can't answer you. He can't do four-dimensional differential calculus. He can't quantify string theory. He can't calculate pi to ten duotrigintillion digits. He can't —"

Kyle switched off Erasmus. Sometimes you wanted to talk to someone who couldn't answer.

At school the next day, Kyle watched what had by now become a daily ritual: the Seating of Mighty Mike.

Everyone wanted to be at Mike's table for lunch. Riots threatened to break out every day at noon when Mike marched into the lunchroom. So the teachers came up with a schedule. Each day, Mike would sit at a different table with a different group of kids.

It was, Kyle thought, a colossal waste of time and the very limited brainpower of the teachers at Bouring Middle School. They could have just ordered Mike to eat somewhere else, preferably the moon. Problem solved.

Today was the day he would sit at Mairi's table. Kyle normally ate with Mairi.

Kyle went through the lunch line. The cheeseburger appeared to be the selection least likely to contain any sort of dangerous bacteria or germs, so he chose that. The French fries were probably okay, too, having been doused in boiling fat. He skipped the salad because it was wilted and looked like it had been sneezed on repeatedly.

Mairi's jaw dropped in shock when Kyle sat down next to her.

"What — what are you doing here?" she asked.

"Eating lunch," he said.

"Yeah, but . . ."

"What?"

Mairi glanced at the three other kids at the table. Kyle knew them all and smiled and nodded his head pleasantly. They ignored him, watching the opening from the lunch line as if the answers to life would emerge.

She leaned over to him. "Today's the day Mike eats at this table. I thought you would . . ."

"Would what?"

"I know you don't like him —"

"Don't like him? Where did you get *that* idea?"

Mairi stared at him.

"Oh, I admit I'm not some Mike worshipper like everyone else in this town, but that doesn't mean I don't like him. I like him fine. He's —"

A cheer went up, drowning out whatever Kyle would have said next. Mike had deigned to manifest himself from the lunch line. When he wasn't wearing his costume, he looked like any other kid, but they applauded and hollered like he was the president.

He sat down across from Kyle, the only remaining place at the table.

Just as Kyle had planned.

"Hi, Mike," Kyle said, forcing himself to smile.

Mike's eyes widened and he smiled back. "Hi! You're Kyle, right? We haven't talked since that day we played football." He leaned across the table to shake Kyle's hand.

Kyle kept smiling and shook that powerful hand, resisting the urge to show Mike his own strength. "Not football. Soccer."

"Really? Are you sure? I think we used our feet. And I know there was a ball."

"Trust me. It's soccer."

"I don't remember there being any socks."

"Seriously. Just trust me."

Mighty Mike sat back, a thoughtful look on his face. "I believe you," he said at last.

"Well, I'm right, so that's good." Before Mairi could chide him for being sarcastic, he said, "I hope you're liking things here in Bouring."

"I am! It's a very friendless town."

"I think you mean 'friendly,'" Mairi chimed in.

Mike tilted his head back and looked at the ceiling, then nodded triumphantly. "Yes. Friendly. Thank you."

The other three kids at the table didn't bother talking — they just stared at Mike in rapt adoration.

"Have the authorities had any luck finding your parents?" Mairi asked, her voice so full of concern that Kyle wanted to tell her to cough it up before she choked on it.

"Not yet. They've been very busy. My printerfinger is not in the system, apparently."

"Fingerprints," Kyle said helpfully.

Mike frowned for a moment, thinking. "Yes. Fingerprints. Of course. That makes more sense."

"How's that brain damage coming along?" Kyle asked.

"Kyle!" Mairi smacked his shoulder and he had to pretend to feel it. "I can't believe you!"

"What? He's got brain damage. Everyone knows it."

"It's rude to say it like that. He's not brain damaged. He's just . . ." She pursed her lips, trying to think of a better word. "He's just not in his right mind. Oops." She clapped a hand over her mouth. "That's worse!"

"It's all right, Mairi," Mike said gently. "My brain is, in fact, not totally up to velocity. It's a cider feck of the meteor radiation. But I'm getting better every day." He smiled at Kyle. "Thanks for asking."

"I think you meant 'side effect' back there," Kyle said, trying to sound helpful. The fact that Mike could take an insult and just blink and pretend it hadn't happened was driving him nuts. He wanted to get under this kid's skin, but Mike was so nice it was creepy. "So, your fingerprints are no good, but have they tried DNA?" He wondered what alien DNA looked like.

"Also not in the system," Mike said. "Oh, look. That's a cool Poddy." He pointed to Erasmus, which Kyle had positioned on the table.

"It's not a Poddy. It's . . ." Kyle sighed. Mike's brain damage/amnesia was exhausting. "My parents gave him, I mean it, to me," Kyle said.

"Can I see it?"

Kyle's brain raced. He had made some modifications to Erasmus last night. In fact, that was the only reason he had voluntarily plopped into a seat with an unobstructed view of Mighty Mike.

Because right now, Erasmus was sending out an invisible beam that was scanning Mighty Mike's body.

If he let Mighty Mike actually hold Erasmus, Erasmus could glean even more information. But it was risky. What if Mike realized there was something abnormal about Erasmus?

"Sure," Kyle said. "Go ahead." He handed Erasmus over, thinking, *You better behave, Erasmus!*

Mairi couldn't believe what she was seeing. Kyle shrugged at the expression on her face, then kept on smiling as Mike slipped Erasmus's earbuds in and turned him on. Fortunately, Erasmus had the good sense to pretend to be nothing more than a music player.

But the whole time, Kyle knew, Mike's brain was being analyzed. . . .

Mike tossed his head back and forth in time to music that only he could hear. "I love the hoppity-hip music!"

"Hip-hop," every single person at the table (even the quiet kids) said at the same time.

"Kyle!" Mairi said. "Why are you giggling?"

Oops. That was out loud? "Nothing. Just . . . thought of something funny."

As he watched his hated enemy rock out with Erasmus, Kyle thought of a great many funny things.

All of them involved Mighty Mike . . . gone forever.

from the top secret journal of
Kyle Camden (deciphered):

The risk was worth it! Oh, what a glorious day this has been!

Ever since the fiasco that was Mighty Mike Day, I've been spending most of my time in the basement, converting it to my own permanent laboratory. (It's coming along quite well, BTW. The miniature nuclear reactor is almost online, and my biochemical forge plans look good.)

But as much progress as I've made down there . . . I haven't come any closer to destroying Mike.

Until now.

Erasmus scanned every last inch of that brat's alien physique. While Mike was listening to music and rocking out, Erasmus was recording samples of his alien brain waves.

Now, unfortunately, I don't yet have a computer system that can decode all of this information. But I'm working on one. In the meantime, I at least have some information.

I also have some data on the radiation in Mike's body, the same radiation in my body. The radiation from the plasma storm.

I've built a machine that just analyzes this radiation. Maybe, in time, I can learn how to remove Mike's powers. Or increase mine. Or both.

You have to know your enemy to defeat your enemy, after all.

CHAPTER
EIGHTEEN

By the weekend, Kyle was more aggravated than before. And considering how aggravated he was earlier, that was a whole new level of aggravation. (He still hadn't invented a word to describe this new level of aggravation. It was on his to-do list, though. Right under "travel through time.")

He spent all of his free time in the laboratory he'd built in the basement. The time machine sat half finished in the corner. (It didn't look like a time machine; it looked like Dad's old motorbike. That's mainly because it *was* Dad's old motorbike, with lots of special, hidden modifications.)

His MiMiRDAA (Mighty Mike Radiation Detector And Analyzer) sat on a corner of the workbench, quietly grinding away, thinking to itself. He'd built it into an ancient cell phone that was almost as big as the cordless upstairs. (How had people ever carried those things around? Where did they keep them? Did they have gigantic pockets back then?)

But even though he was making progress, he still felt no closer to destroying Mighty Mike. He needed something big. He needed . . .

He needed the World's Most Perfect Prank.

That was it! That's what would finally destroy Mighty Mike! Kyle had been spending so much time trying to think of ways to hurt Mike that he'd forgotten the easiest way. He had to go back to basics, back to the pranks that had made him so successful in the past. Mike loved the adoration he received from the world. But if Kyle could pull a prank that would get the public to see Mike for what he was . . . If he could push Mike to the edge and make Mike lose his cool . . .

If he could manage that, then Mighty Mike would self-destruct. He would show his true colors and the world would turn against him.

Only with the World's Most Perfect Prank would he push Mike to the limit, tormenting him beyond his superhuman endurance. And so the world would learn that Mighty Mike was just as mundane and boring and unworthy of attention as everything else out there. He had to play to his strengths.

But Kyle couldn't come up with anything. Nothing. No one could find Mike's real family (and only Kyle knew they never would because his real family was from some other planet), but the people of Bouring had gotten used to having a real-life superhero in their midst. No one was looking very hard anymore.

Meanwhile, every day that Kyle didn't develop the World's Most Perfect Prank was a day when Mighty Mike made more and more friends at school. A day for Mighty Mike to patrol the skies of Bouring, saving kittens from trees, stopping car accidents, helping little old ladies cross the street.

"Kittens in trees . . ." Kyle mumbled. He was sitting in bed with Lefty on his lap, stroking the rabbit's soft fur. It relaxed him. "Kittens in trees . . ." Erasmus was playing some soothing music. Tibetan chants. Or something like that.

"Wait a minute!" Kyle shouted, sitting upright, scaring Lefty, who hopped off of him and retreated to the other side of the bed. "Kittens in trees! That's it!"

"What is it?" Erasmus interrupted the peaceful chanting.

"I've got the World's Most Perfect Prank! It's so simple! So obvious!" He rolled onto his stomach and pulled Lefty over so that they were nose-to-nose. "Listen, Lefty — it's easy. Mike's always out there saving people, right? And just the other day he rescued a lost dog out by the lighthouse. And last week he swooped out of nowhere to get a cat out of a tree."

"Where are you going with this?"

"Shut up, Erasmus. I'm talking to Lefty. Look, this will be easy. The best plans are usually the simplest ones, right? So I'll get a cat. Then I'll *clone* the cat. And do some genetic modifications. Change its DNA, you know? I'll make a cat that sticks to trees no matter what! No matter how much Mike pulls, that cat isn't going *any-where*. He can pull all day and all night. Eventually, he'll just pull up the tree by the roots! He'll look like an idiot!"

Kyle started laughing — it was loud and sustained. Lefty hopped off the bed and ran back into his cage. Mom opened his bedroom door and poked her head in. "What's so funny?" she asked, her left eyelid twitching like crazy.

"Nothing!" Kyle said between gasps, rolling on the bed. "Nothing!"

Mom left, her eyelid still twitching, her shoulder occasionally jerking for no reason at all.

Kyle finally managed to catch his breath. "So. What do you think of *that* plan, Erasmus?"

"Honestly? I think you need some sort of therapy. Talking therapy, maybe. Or —"

"Shut up."

"— maybe adjunct therapy. You know, learn an instrument. Paint a sunset."

"Erasmus."

"Or maybe just plain old electroconvulsive therapy. It's amazing how relaxing eight hundred milliamps of electricity can be when applied properly —"

"I hate you."

"You based me on yourself, Kyle. Which means that you hate yourself. Exactly the sort of thing a good therapist would —"

"*Gah!*" He reached for the off switch.

"No, wait!" Erasmus said. "Don't turn me off again. Really. Let me help you. That's why you made me."

Kyle sighed. That was true. He closed Lefty's cage and dropped in a yogurt treat. "Okay. So help."

"You have to drop the cat thing. Really. Think about it. First of all, where would you get the cat? A pet store? Then you're stuck with a pet cat that you don't want. And Lefty doesn't like cats."

This, too, was true. Lefty had been known to attack cats. He was an unusually aggressive and brave rabbit.

"I don't really need the whole cat. Just some DNA to clone it from. I could just go get some fur from —"

"Fine. Assume you get the cat DNA. What then? The biochemical forge isn't ready yet — you still need some perchloroethylene and dihydrogen monoxide. At the very least. *And* you have to get the nuclear reactor running in order to power it."

All true.

"I have an idea, though," Erasmus said. "It's very sneaky. You'll like it."

Kyle leaned closer to Lefty's cage, watching the rabbit's nose twitch as he chomped his way through the yogurt treat. As Erasmus explained his plan, Kyle smiled a slow, deliberate smile.

CHAPTER NINETEEN

Mairi called him a few moments later. "Aren't you pick-ing me up?" she asked.

"Picking you up?" Kyle asked.

"Did you forget?"

"Of course not," Kyle lied, then covered the phone with one hand. "What did I forget?" he asked Erasmus.

"Astronomy Club," Erasmus reminded him.

"Right." He uncovered the phone. "I totally did not forget about Astronomy Club. I was just leav-ing now."

"Okay."

He hung up. He *had* forgotten about Astronomy Club. But this was actually a good opportunity for him. After all, Mighty Mike patrolled the skies every night at this time, often ranging far beyond Bouring to lend a hand in neighboring towns. This meant that Kyle would get some time alone with Mairi, time to see if he couldn't coax her into seeing Mike for what he truly was.

"Don't forget the costume," Erasmus reminded him.

The costume. Right. That was part of the plan. Erasmus's genius plan. (Which meant it was really Kyle's genius plan, since Erasmus *was* Kyle, in a manner of speaking.)

The plan was utterly simple and completely flawless, like all good plans.

Basically, Kyle needed to become a hero.

It was simple. He would dress as the Azure Avenger and do some sort of good deed. People would begin to admire him. Then, it would be a simple matter to goad Mighty Mike into attacking him. After all, Mike had viciously attacked him on Mighty Mike Day, when Kyle was just trying to shut down the Pants Laser. It would be easy to make Mike attack him.

And when people saw Mike attack their beloved Azure Avenger, they would turn on him.

Simple.

So Kyle tossed his costume into his backpack, along with some snacks. At the last minute, he decided to take his MiMiRDAA with him, too. (It needed a shorter name, he decided. From now on, he would just call it MiMi.)

He slung the backpack over one shoulder and walked down the street to Mairi's house. The night was cool and crisp — a perfect fall evening. The sky was cloudless. It would be a great night for stargazing.

Mairi's house was only a couple of blocks away, on the way to school. Kyle knocked at the front door. As always, he was amused by the sign out front that read, VISIT THE HISTORIC BOURING LIGHTHOUSE! and had directions and information about visiting hours. Mairi's mom just wouldn't give up on that lighthouse.

Mairi opened the door. "I'm glad you didn't forget," she said as they walked toward school.

"How could I forget this?"

"Can you take your earbuds out? It's rude to listen to music while we're talking."

Kyle took out Erasmus's buds and tucked him away in his backpack. "Sorry."

"You wear them all the time now. What's so amazing that you're listening to it so much?"

"Uh . . . It's an audiobook about Cagliostro. He was this trickster in the —"

"You and your pranks." She sighed, her breath a tiny plume on the night air. "When are you going to give up that stuff?"

Kyle bristled. Mairi understood how important his pranks were to him. "I don't do them for *me*, you know. I do them to —"

"— to show the world how silly it is so that people will shape up. I know. I just wonder . . . Isn't there another way to do that?"

"Like what?"

"I don't know. Lead by example, maybe?"

Kyle stiffened. "Like Mighty Mike, you mean?"

Mairi shrugged. "Why are you so jealous of him?"

"I'm not."

"I can totally hear it in your voice."

"Can not."

"Can so."

They walked in silence for a few moments.

"Maybe a tiny bit jealous," Kyle admitted, for reasons he didn't quite understand.

"You don't have to be, Kyle. No one expects you to be Mighty Mike. You're you. That's what matters."

It was the sort of thing a parent or a teacher would say, but for some reason, when Mairi said it, Kyle *didn't* want to throw up.

At the school, they went around back to the football field, which was bordered on one side by a massive cornfield that stretched as far as the eye could see. A chill ran through Kyle. He hadn't been here since the night of the plasma storm. And now here he was with ten other kids and two teachers, gazing up at the stars. . . .

Which one did Mighty Mike hail from? Kyle wondered. Of the millions of stars in the universe, around which one spun the planet Mike called home? What were the people like there? Why had they sent Mighty Mike here? What was his real mission? What was he up to on Earth?

He shivered and tossed his backpack on the ground next to Mairi, who was already lying on her back, looking up into the sky. Kyle sat cross-legged next to her and craned his neck. He tuned out Miss Schwartz, who was pointing out Ursa Major and Mars and Cassiopeia and the Big Dipper. Kyle knew the stars very well already.

"Where's Pegasus?" Mairi whispered.

Kyle pointed. "There."

"I don't see it."

Kyle lay back and took her hand. "Here. I'll show you." He pointed her finger. "That's called Markab. It's the alpha star in Pegasus. They call it Alpha Peg. Then you trace down to this one here — Scheat. It's the Beta Peg. And you go this way and you see the wings, see?"

Mairi smiled. "I see it now. Thanks."

He let go of her hand.

"I love the story of Pegasus," she said. "I like that even though Bellerophon did something wrong and was punished, Zeus didn't punish his horse. And Pegasus got a job as Zeus's horse, which is cool."

Kyle snorted. "Bellerophon was just trying to put Zeus in his place. Zeus overreacted."

"You *would* think that."

Kyle sat up. Miss Schwartz was blathering about Mars, getting most of her information wrong. Kyle wished he had brought some glowing putty. He'd whipped up a batch the other night. It would have been fun to spread the stuff around and have Miss Schwartz try to explain what it was.

"Are we going to get hit by meteors?" asked a little kid. Some Astronomy Club members had brought younger brothers and sisters.

"No, that's over with," Miss Schwartz said.

And they weren't meteors anyway, Kyle thought. *Plasma curtain, people! Plasma!* Yeah, the glowing putty would have been perfect. . . .

"Did you bring anything to eat?" Mairi asked. "You said you would."

"Yep," Kyle said absently, still imagining what he could do with the glowing putty. "In my backpack."

Mairi rolled over and grabbed Kyle's backpack, dragging it over to her. She unzipped the big pouch.

Kyle spun around at superspeed, not even aware he was doing it. If anyone had been watching him in that moment, they would have seen only a vaguely Kyle-shaped and Kyle-colored blur in the air.

"No!" he shouted to Mairi. "Don't!"

He was so loud that everyone turned to look. "Kyle, please keep it down for those students who *do* want to hear what I have to say!" said Miss Schwartz.

Kyle didn't care about Miss Schwartz and her lecture or the other students. He didn't care about anything right now except for the fact that Mairi was about to look inside his backpack.

Where he'd stuffed his Azure Avenger costume.

"Don't go in my backpack," Kyle told her.

Mairi was frozen, the backpack open in her lap, one hand poised to peel back the flap. "What is *with* you, Kyle?"

Kyle's brain could calculate the movement of atoms, the density of alloys, the speed of lava running downhill, and the number of kittens born in a three-mile radius in the past ten minutes (ninety-seven — go figure), but at that moment, his superpowerful brain couldn't come up with a reason for Mairi *not* to look in his backpack. Other than the truth, of course. Which totally was not an option.

"I — My —" he stammered. Oh, sure — *that* was brilliant.

"You forgot the food, didn't you?" Mairi said. "I can't believe it. You said you would bring snacks."

"Right. I know. I forgot. I screwed up. I'm sorry." There were six candy bars, a baggie full of peanuts, two small bags of potato chips, a plastic container of carrots, and two yogurt tubes in his backpack, but he wasn't about to tell *her* that.

Mairi sighed. "Fine. I'll go see if anyone else has anything."

She tossed the backpack aside, stood, brushed grass and dirt off her pants, and marched up the hill to where Miss Schwartz and the other students had wandered.

Whew! That was *close*!

Kyle couldn't believe how he'd almost had his identity exposed! He couldn't just carry his costume around in his backpack. It was too risky. He would need to come up with a better solution.

He dug into the backpack and pulled out the food, spreading it on the ground in front of him, then zipped up the backpack securely. When Mairi came back, he would say that — *Oops! Dummy me!* — he'd forgotten that he *had* packed food after all. *Sorry about that, Mairi. So silly of me . . .*

A little ways away, Mairi turned back to him and waved, just to show there were no hard feelings.

Kyle waved back and then returned to the food, arranging it on the ground so that it looked like a gourmet spread. He'd done a good job packing, he thought.

"Oh, my God!" Miss Schwartz screamed. At the same time, a chorus of shrieks and cries went up from the other students.

Kyle looked up. A second ago, Mairi had been maybe ten yards away from him, about halfway between him and the group on the hill. Now she was . . .

She was *gone*.

And in her place was a giant sinkhole.

Kyle blinked. What had —

Just then, the sinkhole erupted, a geyser of dirt and

rocks and grass fountaining up into the sky. And in that geyser . . .

Mairi.

She screamed. Miss Schwartz screamed — again. Everyone, basically, screamed.

Except for Kyle.

Spontaneous earth eruption? he thought. *That's impossible!*

The geyser twisted and rotated in the air. Mairi struggled, but bands of soil had wrapped around her and now dragged her out of the sky and back underground.

It was alive. The ground was *alive*.

CHAPTER
TWENTY

Kyle stared, but only for a second. He didn't have much time. How long could Mairi survive underground, without air?

Not long. He could calculate it exactly. Take her lung capacity, based on her size. . . . Consider that she had been screaming a moment ago. . . . Multiply. Divide. . . .

He decided he didn't want to know. It would be a small number. A small amount of time Mairi had left to live.

He grabbed the backpack. Everyone was busy watching the sinkhole, so no one saw him run at top speed toward the cornfield, where the tall stalks hid him from sight. He switched clothes in less than two seconds, plugging in Erasmus.

"Don't forget MiMi," Erasmus said immediately.

Right. MiMi. Of course. This couldn't be a coincidence. The ground just wouldn't *happen* to open up and come alive here. This field was where the plasma storm hit. The same radiation that powered Mighty Mike —

the same radiation that powered *Kyle* — had to be causing this. MiMi might be able to help.

Kyle launched himself into the sky, MiMi clutched in one hand. Her screen lit up. Data streamed across it.

Just then, the ground belched again. Mairi hurtled up into the air, almost as high as Kyle, surrounded by tendrils of soil and rock. She screamed again, struggling and writhing against the earthy tentacles that gripped her.

Down below, kids gathered in a group pointed up at him. "Look!" someone shouted. "The Blue Freak!"

"It's the Azure Avenger," Kyle muttered under his breath. He clipped MiMi to his belt and dived straight at the heaviest, thickest tendril of dirt.

SMACK! The tendril undulated, crashing against Kyle. It was like being hit with a brick wall. An angry brick wall.

Kyle shook his head. Other than being punched by Mighty Mike, he hadn't felt pain since his exposure to the plasma storm. And now.

He decided he didn't like it.

He marshaled all his strength and flew at the tendril again. It whipped around. Mairi somehow found the breath and the energy to scream once more.

Kyle plowed right through the tendril, severing it. Now Mairi was only held by two other tendrils.

He pulled up and spun around, breathing hard, satisfied by his success —

Oh. Oh, no.

The tendril re-formed almost instantly, more dirt flowing up from the ground.

Kyle gritted his teeth. How could he —?

Just then he noticed something: The dirt was changing its direction. It was flowing *down* now. It was collapsing back toward the ground again. . . .

"Stop screaming!" he yelled at Mairi. "Hold your breath!"

She looked at him, her eyes wide with terror. At the last possible instant, she closed her mouth, just as the tendril once again collapsed into a sinkhole, dragging Mairi underground.

Kyle itched to blast a path through the soil, tunneling down to find Mairi. But he stopped himself. That was no good. He didn't know where she was under there, how close to the surface. With his speed and strength, he could smash through the ground . . . and right through Mairi, if he wasn't careful.

Besides, brute force wasn't how Kyle did things. He had to use his brain, not his brawn. He wasn't Mighty Mike, after all.

Even though he knew Mairi's life was slipping away with every moment he did nothing, he forced himself to think as he hovered over the sinkhole and the group of kids who had been ushered away by Miss Schwartz. They all pointed up at him like this was his fault.

He unclipped MiMi from his belt. "Give me some good news," he said.

"MiMi can't talk," Erasmus reminded him. "She doesn't have an artificial —"

"Shut up, Erasmus. Or I'll toss you into orbit. I'm serious."

Erasmus shut up.

MiMi's screen lit up with data. Kyle read it as quickly as it came up, calculating. . . .

He was right. This wasn't a coincidence. The sinkhole was chock-full of the same radiation in Mighty Mike's body. The radiation in Kyle's body.

The radiation from the plasma storm.

Worse yet . . .

Wait. How long had Mairi been underground? Less than thirty seconds so far. She was probably still alive, as long as she was still holding her breath. . . .

Stop thinking about that, Kyle! She needs you to focus on figuring this out!

The radiation wasn't just in the area of the sinkhole. There was a radiation trail from the spot where Mairi vanished, leading all the way to the exact spot where Mike touched down during the plasma storm.

And now . . . he calculated fiercely. This couldn't be. . . . It wasn't possible!

But it was.

According to MiMi and Kyle's own calculations, the lingering radiation from the plasma storm was spreading. The sinkhole was only the beginning. Soon the "living soil" would be everywhere . . . and the entire town of Bouring would be in danger!

And then, maybe . . . the world.

CHAPTER
TWENTY-ONE

For a single, terrible second, Kyle couldn't move. Couldn't think. Couldn't do anything at all.

The enormity of it was stronger than anything he'd encountered yet. The entire world could be in danger.

Why was this happening *now*? It was awfully convenient that it happened *right* when Kyle was around. . . .

Unless . . . unless maybe he somehow triggered it? He hadn't been to the field since the plasma storm. Maybe the radiation in his body somehow activated the lingering radiation in the ground. . . .

It didn't matter! He had to do something. But what?

Below him, the group of kids started applauding and cheering and generally going nuts. But Kyle hadn't even done anything yet.

Then he saw the true object of their affections: Mighty Mike swooped in from the east, just as the sinkhole erupted again, spitting Mairi up into the air, still snared within tendrils of dirt and rock. She looked exhausted beyond all belief, but Kyle could tell that she was still breathing.

"*Now* what have you done?" Mike asked as he blew past Kyle on his way to Mairi.

"I didn't —" But Mike was already out of earshot.

Of *course* Mike would blame him. . . .

Kyle watched as Mike had exactly as much success fighting the dirt monster as Kyle had. In other words, none. The tendrils batted Mike around, all while deftly maneuvering Mairi out of the way every time Mike came close to snatching her from their clutches.

Police cars and fire trucks rumbled onto the scene, their sirens blaring and obnoxious.

You idiots, Kyle thought, hovering above them all. *You can't shoot dirt. And all your hoses will do is make it mud. Morons.*

If this was going to be resolved, it would have to be resolved by Kyle.

While Mairi was aboveground, she could breathe, and that meant Kyle could think without panicking. He made a slow, deliberate circle around the tendrils, keeping MiMi pointed down at the source of the radiation, scanning. He needed as much information as possible in order to think his way out of this.

Just then, Mike broke off his attack and did something that Kyle had to admit was slightly smart: Instead of attacking the tendrils directly, he dive-bombed them at their source, plunging directly into the ground.

Kyle kept scanning, but he kept an eye on the crowd

below. They were all watching in silent amazement as the ground bucked and rippled where Mike had tunneled in. The cops and firefighters were pulling kids away from the area and setting up a perimeter, as if that would help once the radiation spread to the ground under their feet . . . and beyond.

The ground exploded into a roiling wave of earth. Mike came streaking out of the ground like a bottle rocket, tumbling head over heels through the air. More soil was coming alive and fighting back.

After getting his bearings, Mike drifted over to Kyle, mud and dirt streaming off of him. His face was black with soil, his eyes bright white stamps.

"Look, whatever you're doing, you have to stop it," he told Kyle. "That's an innocent girl over there."

Kyle waved him off. He was too busy thinking. The radiation was fanning out at a geometric progression. If he didn't hurry, pretty soon the whole area around the school would be engulfed. And it would keep going.

"Erasmus, start thinking about what we would need to do to clean up this radiation, okay?"

"Right."

Mighty Mike came closer. "Did you hear me? Whatever grudge you have against me, fine. But don't take it out on innocent people."

"Look, punk. I don't have time to mess with you, okay? I'm busy. There's a radiation —"

"Give me that thing," Mike ordered, pointing at MiMi.

Kyle drifted back a couple of feet, cradling MiMi protectively. "Forget it. No. You can't have her."

"You're using that thing to control the ground. I've been watching."

"No, I'm using her to analyze —"

Mike burst forward, getting in Kyle's face before Kyle could react. "Give it to me!"

Kyle batted Mike's hand away, holding MiMi out so that Mike couldn't grab her. "Get back, you idiot! I'm trying to help!"

"You're going to kill that girl and who knows how many other people!"

Mike spun around Kyle, reaching out for MiMi again. Kyle pulled her back just in time.

"I don't have time for you, Mike. I'm trying to save her life! And maybe everyone on the planet, too!"

"I've seen what happens when you lose control of your toys. Hand it over and let me fix things. Again."

Kyle punched him.

He hadn't meant to. It just sort of happened. His temper had been flaring the whole time because Mike was distracting him when he was trying to save Mairi's life.

Right now she was still aboveground, but the sinkhole could recollapse at any second. And this time she might not come back. He didn't have time to debate with an inferior intellect.

So he punched Mike right in the face, sending him careering through the air. The crowd booed.

"I have some thoughts . . ." Erasmus said.

"Give me a second," Kyle said. "But keep talking." He clipped MiMi to his belt again and made himself a missile, headed straight at Mike. Before Mike could recover from the sucker punch, Kyle body slammed him at Mach 1.

He hated to admit it, but it felt good to pound Mighty Mike. So he hit him again, punching him right in the face.

"You idiot!" he railed. "You moron! You ignoramus!" And then he threw in some really bad words, mostly ones Dad had used last summer when he'd slammed his fingers in the freezer door.

"I'm trying to help and you won't get off my back, you jerk!"

Mighty Mike blocked the next punch, his teeth bared, his eyes alight with anger. "You wouldn't know how to help if your life depended on it."

"Bite me," Kyle said, and kicked Mike between the legs. Then he grabbed Mike by that stupid cape, swung him around in a circle, and let go, tossing him toward the water tower.

"That's gonna be wet," Erasmus said.

"Don't care. Don't have time for him. We're outta here." He put on the speed and flew off toward his house, moving so quickly that he'd just be a tiny blur to anyone watching.

"Far be it from me to judge you," Erasmus said, "but Mairi's still in danger and —"

"We have a bigger problem than that. Mike won't let anything happen to Mairi. That's the one good thing about do-gooder punks — they're dependable. But in the meantime, someone has to figure out how to stop the radiation from spreading and save the whole world!"

"Oh," Erasmus said. "That. Right."

CHAPTER
TWENTY-TWO

The flight home took less than a minute, so Erasmus talked fast, keeping up a steady stream of ideas, suggestions, and plans. By the time Kyle had flown through the basement door, he already had the schematics designed in his head.

He moved through his lab at top speed. Unfortunately, he had to dismantle the partly completed nuclear reactor and the time machine; he needed the parts.

"Kyle!" his mother yelled from the top of the basement stairs. "What is all that racket?"

"Nothing, Mom!" He prayed that she wouldn't come downstairs and see him in his Azure Avenger outfit. He really didn't want to zap her brain again.

"Try to keep it down! Your father and I are watching TV."

Of course you're watching TV. What else would you be doing?

"I'll try!" He pried open MiMi's case and gingerly connected her battery terminals to the portable dampening rod he'd scavenged from the nuclear reactor. If he slipped, he would probably blow up the house and let loose a cloud of radioactive particles that would kill everything in the county.

"No pressure," Erasmus whispered.

"Shut up."

"Shutting up."

Kyle teased the wires together, sweat gathering under his mask. No biggie. Only life on Earth hung in the balance. Nothing to worry about.

Success! He had the dampening rod connected and nothing had blown up.

"Good job," Erasmus said, sounding serious for the first time ever.

"It's your design," Kyle told him. "I just built it."

"Let's hope it works."

Kyle threw open the basement door and blazed into the sky. Then he broke the sound barrier again, heading back to school.

And the field.

And Mairi.

Mighty Mike thrashed in the grips of the living ground. There now more tendrils than before, and they were larger and stronger. The area of danger had grown dramatically, spreading out to the perimeter the police and firefighters had established. As Kyle neared the field, he noticed the cops beginning to move their equipment and personnel back. They were just beginning to get an inkling as to what was really going on here.

But they didn't seem *too* worried. They trusted Mighty Mike.

Pinheads.

You can't beat up the ground. Duh.

Mairi was still alive, still struggling and screaming as Mike tried to fight his way through the endlessly shifting columns of earth. Occasionally he would blast forth with a beam of black, laserlike light from his eyes. It sliced neatly through the dirt, but the tendrils just re-formed moments later.

The enhanced MiMi showed the radiation slowly leaching throughout the ground, spreading. But it was most concentrated just over the hill, at the exact spot where Kyle had seen Mighty Mike touch down on Earth for the first time.

He would have to start there.

He darted over the hill, moving so fast that no one could see. Not that they would have noticed him even if he had ambled calmly up the grade in full view of everyone — the entire crowd was captivated by Mighty Mike's useless combat with the living ground.

Kyle hovered over the spot where Mighty Mike had landed. He punched in a new code on MiMi's ancient cell phone pad.

"Wait a second," Erasmus said. "Think about what you're doing."

"I can't think long. Any minute now, the ground around the school will become alive, too."

"This is an opportunity to have a sample of the radiation in its purest form. Without Mighty Mike's DNA or your DNA complicating things."

That was true, Kyle had to admit.

He spared a moment and skimmed the ground quickly, scooping up some of the dirt. He dumped it into a belt pouch. MiMi whined and chittered at her proximity to the radioactive soil.

"Okay, now to get to work!"

He flew straight up so that he had a good vantage point. Then he pointed MiMi at the ground. Her antenna had been replaced with the dampening rod and a bewildering array of wires.

"I hope this works better than the Pants Laser," Erasmus said.

For once, Kyle agreed with Erasmus.

He punched in another series of numbers on the keypad and MiMi began to hum.

"Is it working?" Erasmus asked.

"I don't know. Too soon to tell. MiMi's dampening antenna should be causing the radiation to decouple from —"

"I know how she works. I designed her."

"You *helped*."

"I did all the hard work."

"Oh, yeah? How did you put her together without any hands, you hunk of electro —"

He broke off as MiMi's screen scrolled data. It was working!

As he watched, the alien radiation in the ground below him was slowly dissipating, thanks to MiMi's dampening antenna. Kyle held her steady, aiming her at the spot with the greatest concentration of radiation.

"Connect me to her data port," Erasmus said. "I can monitor the radiation directly."

Kyle fumbled for a cable. Erasmus was wireless, but he hadn't had time to install Wi-Fi in MiMi's rickety old shell.

Once Erasmus was plugged in, it got easier. Kyle could focus on keeping MiMi aimed steadily at the right spot while Erasmus fed him a stream of information and adjustments. MiMi started to buck in Kyle's hands and he struggled to hold her still.

"He's winning!" someone shouted.

Kyle looked around, but he was still alone. What —?

"Go, Mighty Mike! Kick its butt!"

The crowd down the hill started chanting its hero's name.

"As you weaken the source of the radiation, it's weakening all over," Erasmus said. "So —"

"The dirt monster is getting its butt handed to it by Mighty Mike. Yeah, thanks, I figured that part out."

"MiMi's shielding is breaking down!" Erasmus was starting to sound panicked. "She can't keep this up much longer."

Kyle gritted his teeth. "Come on, baby. Hold together."

"Kyle! You need to adjust the resequencing engine or —"

"I got it!" Kyle tapped at the keypad with his thumbs, texting the codes that would save the world.

MiMi adjusted her dampeners.

"The radiation level here is almost back to normal! It's almost —"

A cheer exploded from down the hill. Kyle spared a glance in that direction. The dirt monster collapsed in a shower of soil and rocks as Mighty Mike delivered a massive, powerful blow to the heart of the creature.

"You've decontaminated the area. Now the radiation that spread down the hill is being sucked up."

"Yeah. No kidding." He watched as Mairi dropped out of the sky. Every fiber of his being wanted to swoop in and catch her, but all he could do was watch as

Mike — to more cheers — plucked her safely out of the air.

"Kyle! Kyle!" Erasmus, sounding even more panicked now. "MiMi can't take the strain! You have to do something!"

Kyle swept his glance over the screen. The radiation was practically gone now. "Another minute," he said.

"In another minute, she'll blow up!"

Kyle held her steady. "Good girl," he said. "Good girl."

Sweat dripped into his eyes under his mask. He blinked rapidly to clear his vision, staring at the screen. Just another ten seconds. Nine. Eight.

"Kyle!"

The radiation was gone. Completely gone.

Kyle unplugged Erasmus and hurled MiMi into the sky as hard and as fast as he could. The explosion was minor. If you weren't looking for it, you never would have noticed, so only Kyle and Erasmus watched as MiMi died to save the world.

For once, neither of them had anything to say. They hung in the air, silent, hovering.

And then Kyle heard Sheriff Monroe over a police bullhorn: "Spread out! The Blue Freak is believed to be in the area still! His monster has been stopped, but he's still on the loose!"

"My monster? *My* monster? That imbecilic, microbrained —"

"Also," the bullhorn went on, "a student is missing. Please be on the lookout for Kyle Camden, who may have been injured by the monster. . . ."

Kyle stopped listening. He *was* missing! And conveniently, the Blue Freak (Azure Avenger! Azure Avenger! *Grr* — now they had *him* doing it!) had appeared. He had to get back quickly before anyone became suspicious. Or found his backpack in the cornfield.

He flew back to the cornfield as quickly as he could, staying low to the ground to take advantage of the ground cover. In moments, he'd recovered his backpack. He whipped off his costume at superspeed, then dressed just as fast. Finally, he stumbled out of the cornfield, directly into the brightness of a police officer's flashlight.

"I found him!" the cop yelled.

Kyle allowed the cop to walk him over to an ambulance, where an EMT looked him over before pronouncing him fine. Kyle barely heard the guy. He was busy looking at the ambulance next to his, where Mairi sat on a stretcher, bundled up in a blanket. Her hair and face were filthy and she had three EMTs huddled around her.

He waved to her.

She coughed and nodded to him.

And then — to make the night perfect — Mighty Mike walked up behind her and put a hand on her shoulder.

And Mairi smiled.

CHAPTER
TWENTY-THREE

By the time school started on Monday, the story had spread to everyone, and Mairi had a new nickname: "Mighty Mike's Girlfriend."

"I am so totally *not* his girlfriend," Mairi explained for the thousandth time on the bus that morning. "He saved my life from the Blue Freak's monster and then he just stuck around to make sure I was okay."

"I heard he flew you home," said a kid.

Kyle — sitting next to Mairi, his arms crossed tightly over his chest — fired a beam of pure mental hatred at the kid. If beams of pure mental hatred actually existed, that kid would have been in a world of hurt. Kyle decided to work on pure mental hatred beams. They would be useful.

"Well, yes. He flew me home."

"And I heard your parents made him stay for pie."

Mairi sighed and slouched in the seat. "There was pie."

"There was pie!" someone shouted to the rest of the bus. It passed along the bus like a wave: *There was pie! There was pie! Pie! Pie!*

"What was it like to fly with him?" a kid asked.

"What do his muscles feel like?"

"What does he look like up close?"

"Are his eyes as blue as they look from far away?"

"Did he kiss you good night?"

I'm going to hurt someone, Kyle thought. *It's inevitable.*

"Did he —"

"SHUT UP ALREADY!"

Kyle glowered at everyone. Why were they all staring at him?

Oh, right — *he* was the one who bellowed for everyone to shut up. That's why.

"I, uh, I have a headache," he said, and slumped a bit more in the seat.

"Enough questions," Mairi said. "Leave me alone, okay?"

Between her polite request and Kyle's outburst, the message somehow got through. Kids turned back to their own seats.

"Sorry," Kyle mumbled. "I'm just —"

"— tired of hearing about it. I know. I'm sorry."

"Not your fault they're all idiots. Just because he flew

you home, they think he's your boyfriend." He spat out the last word like it was horse dung coated in battery acid.

Mairi shrugged. "That's not what bothers me."

Kyle vomited in his imagination. How could that *not* bother her?

"What bothers me," she went on, "is that they all treat him like a celebrity or something. He's very lonely. He's just a kid, like us. He just wants friends. He was so happy just to sit in my kitchen and eat pie. You know?"

He's an alien invader who wants to eat our brains. Kyle hoped that was true.

"Yeah. I guess," he said.

"And now that that horrible Blue Freak is around, it's more important than ever that we have Mighty Mike!"

Kyle ground his back teeth. "You know, there's no *proof* that the Blue Freak made the ground come alive. Maybe he —"

"Kyle! Whether he did it or not doesn't matter. He was there and then he *left*. He left me to die! If not for Mike, who knows *what* would have happened?"

Kyle yearned to tell her the truth. He even opened his mouth and had the first sentence ready to roll right off his tongue.

But then he imagined government scientists strapping him down to a table. Studying him. Examining him. Maybe even dissecting him. Who knew?

He was the only person in the world who knew the

truth — the truth about Mighty Mike, the truth about the Blue Freak. The truth about the dirt monster and the way the world had almost ended.

He knew. But there was absolutely nothing he could do with that knowledge. The only one he could tell was Erasmus . . . and Erasmus already knew and didn't care.

Kyle shook his head and closed his mouth and said nothing for the rest of the bus ride.

At school, the Great Nemesis greeted Kyle. Just because his day didn't suck enough already.

"Kyle, if you want to talk about what happened over the weekend . . ."

Kyle rolled his eyes. Did this woman get *paid* for every time she got Kyle into her office? "You know, I wasn't the *only* one there that night, Great Nemesis."

"But Mairi is your best friend. I'm sure it was very frightening to see her in danger. You're a very sensitive child. That's why you ran away into the cornfield when she was in danger. You couldn't bear to watch."

Was *that* what people were saying? That he'd run away? That he was a coward?

Kyle stood up on his toes so that he could glare into the Great Nemesis's eyes. "Listen once and understand me: I did not run away. Kyle Camden does not run from *anything*. Or any*one*. Understood?"

The Great Nemesis took a step back and cleared her throat. When she said nothing, Kyle marched off.

"You're very upset!" she called after him. "I understand. Remember, my office hours are . . ."

Kyle blocked her out.

It got worse in homeroom.

Once again, the principal handed the morning announcements over to Sheriff Monroe. Kyle sat in a stew of misery and disbelief as he listened to what the sheriff had to say:

"I'm sure you all know about what happened over the weekend. If we thought that the Blue Freak was just here the one time on Mighty Mike Day, well, this weekend proved that's not the case. He's here to stay.

"We've been studying all the pictures and video of him. The FBI and the military have been helping, too. We've come to the conclusion that the Blue Freak may be the same age as Mighty Mike. In other words, he may be a kid, just like all of you.

"In fact, he may even live in Bouring. He may even be a student at this school."

Kyle put his head down on the desk as everyone looked around the room in a sudden babble of excitement. Miss Moore shushed them.

"So," Sheriff Monroe went on, "I'm asking all of you to

keep your eyes and ears open. Pay attention. If you see something strange, something that doesn't make sense, maybe someone acting differently . . . If you see something, say something. Report it to your teacher or the administration. Thanks for your time. Have a good day, kids."

Kyle looked up. Mairi was beaming.

"They're finally doing something about him," she breathed. "Maybe they'll catch him and stop him for good."

Kyle put his head down again.

"Kyle? Are you okay? Is it your headache?"

Yeah. He had a headache. And its name was Mighty Mike.

Kyle suffered through school in a daze. As soon as he got home, he headed down to his lab. He still hadn't cleaned up from the other day, when he had blown in here and modified MiMi in a burst of panicked speed.

He started straightening up, trying to organize things as best he could: Parts for the time machine in one corner. Nuclear reactor components on the bottom shelf. Biochemical forge stuff over by the water heater . . .

What was he supposed to do now? Everyone was after him. It wasn't just Mighty Mike and the Great Nemesis and Sheriff Monroe anymore. Now it was the FBI and the army. Heck, the entire United States government!

Then again, the government wasn't really all that good at getting things done as far as Kyle could tell, so maybe that part wasn't a big deal. Still, he didn't like the fact that now every single kid at Bouring Middle School would be watching out for any hint of the Blue Fr — *Azure Avenger*. He would have to be careful. Very careful.

His dad came home from work and came downstairs. "Hey, there, slugger! How — how's it going?"

Kyle made a mental note to poke around inside the brain-wave manipulator and see if he could fix that stutter. And Mom's twitch.

"Fine, Dad."

Kyle wished he could talk to his dad. Granted, his father was — intellectually — as inferior to Kyle as a toad was to a normal human being, but he was older and had more experience in the world. There was a slight chance that Dad might have some sort of insight or advice that Kyle himself couldn't generate with pure brainpower alone.

"What are you up to down here?" Dad asked brightly, looking around.

Kyle stared at the circuit board in his hands. It belonged to the control panel for the biochemical forge.

"School project."

"Great!" Dad said, and slapped Kyle on the shoulder before going back upstairs.

Kyle sighed. He needed to clear his head.

Moments later, he soared over Bouring, staying high enough that anyone looking up would just see a shadow against the night sky. A bird, maybe, or a low-flying plane. He wished he didn't have to wear a full face mask; it had felt nice to have the wind blowing through his hair. He could never fly like that again.

Of course, he'd probably get a lot of bugs in his teeth if he flew around barefaced like that anyway. He wondered how Mighty Mike avoided that, flying around with that stupid face of his hanging out all the time. . . .

He cruised around Bouring once, pausing for a moment over the town square. The park was cordoned off by police tape, the statue of Micah Bouring still lying on its side where Mighty Mike had set it when Kyle had thrown it at the crowd. It was a crime scene, and half the law enforcement officers in a fifty-mile radius spent the days here going over every grain of dirt, looking for something that would help them identify the Blue — the *Azure Avenger.*

Kyle scanned the area quickly. It was past quitting time and no one was around.

He swooped down and grabbed the statue, then lifted it back into place on its damaged pedestal. It was a little wobbly, so he scooped up some gravel and forced it into the gap between the pedestal and the statue until Micah Bouring stood tall and proud.

There.

He took off again before anyone could see him and flew to the outskirts of town, where the lighthouse rose against the night sky. Tonight the main light was on, which meant that Mairi's mom was inside, probably in the cramped office at the top of the lighthouse. Kyle hovered just beyond the railing that ran around the balcony there. He wanted to knock on the door and surprise Mairi's mom, but he didn't.

He wondered what the lighthouse was doing here. He had to admit it was a heck of a mystery, one he'd always wanted to solve. His pranks had occupied most of his thinking time, though, so he'd never gotten around to it. But maybe now that he had so much extra brainpower lying around he could —

"I saw what you did," said a familiar voice.

Kyle spun around.

"To the statue," Mighty Mike said, standing in the air, his hands on his hips. "Putting it back. That was nice. But you messed with a crime scene."

Under his mask, Kyle's cheeks flamed red with embarrassment. He hadn't wanted to be caught doing something nice. "I didn't do it to be nice. I just like imagining the looks on their faces when they come back in the morning and the statue's back in place."

Mike sighed and crossed his arms over his chest, looking very adult all of a sudden. He drifted a little closer to Kyle. "It doesn't have to be like this. Think of all the good we could do together. As partners."

Kyle laughed. "Are you crazy?"

"I just wish you would use your powers for something productive," Mike said.

"Making people realize how silly they are *is* productive."

"Is that what you think you're doing?"

"I know exactly what I'm doing," Kyle said. "What I don't know is what *you're* doing here."

Mike shrugged. "Helping."

"Oh, and that's the only reason you're here? As if we can't survive without you? Somehow the town of Bouring managed to get along before you showed up," Kyle said. "The stalled cars got towed and the kittens got out of trees and the fires got put out and the bad guys got caught. All without you."

Mike grinned. "But I'm better at it."

Kyle clenched his fists. He wanted to punch that grin until there was nothing left of it.

"Now, I saw what you did with the statue," Mike went on. "I know you're not all bad. I could arrest you right now —"

"You can't arrest anything. You're just a kid."

"Didn't you hear? I was deputized by Sheriff Monroe today. After school. I guess you didn't see it on TV."

Deputized? Oh, great. Just what he needed. Bad enough Mike was a punk and a pain in the butt — now he was a punk and a pain in the butt with a *badge*.

Mike's grin widened. "Nothing to say to that? No snappy comeback?"

Kyle wished he'd brought Erasmus with him. Erasmus would have had something to say.

"Just watch yourself," Mike told him. "I would hate to have to fight you again. Because I won't hold back next time."

Kyle seethed. "I saved the entire town the other day. So don't tell me to behave —"

"I would have taken care of things," Mike said, his confidence so blinding and burning that it took every last ounce of willpower for Kyle to resist flying over to him and popping him one.

But the worst thing about that confidence was this: Kyle realized Mike was probably right. So far, Mighty Mike had succeeded at everything he'd attempted.

But he knew one way to hurt Mike. Or at least to show that he knew Mike's weakness:

"I know the truth about you, Mike. I know what you are." He came down hard on the word "what."

Mike didn't even blink. He just shrugged. "Oh? I'm sure you think you know. But maybe I know the truth about *you*, 'Azure Avenger.' Think about that."

Before Kyle could respond, Mike cocked his head to the right. "There's a kid choking on a turkey club sandwich at Dinah's Diner. I'll be right back."

And he sped off to perform yet another annoying good deed, leaving Kyle alone.

I'll be right back, he'd said, as if he expected Kyle to wait for him.

Yeah, right. Typical Mike — he's the important one and everyone else needs to revolve around him.

Not Kyle.

Kyle was no one's lackey. No one's "partner."

Kyle was in charge.

He snorted under his mask and flew home.

He stayed up late, finishing the job organizing his lab. He would need more equipment. More resources. More of everything.

And whatever he had to do to get these things, well . . . he would do.

The last thing he did before going to bed was find a place for the heavy leaded jar with the foil stopper. He'd found it in the crawl space under the basement stairs. Mom had used it when he was younger, when she canned her own fruits and vegetables. It was thick and squat and just the right size to hold the irradiated soil he'd scooped up from the field where Mighty Mike landed.

He put it on an empty shelf. His first trophy in the war against Mighty Mike.

When he was quiet and listened carefully, he could hear a little high-pitched whine from the jar. Sometimes the soil glowed. And sometimes it . . . moved.

He would learn a lot from this handful of dirt, he knew. He would someday find a way to rebuild MiMi. A better MiMi.

Kyle went upstairs. Before he turned off the light, he looked down at his workshop.

Tomorrow was another day. And he had a lot to do.

from the top secret journal of
Kyle Camden (deciphered):

So the forces ranged against me have escalated.

That's all right. They can send the entire Army and Navy and Air Force and the Marines after me. They can send all the cops and agents in the world after me.

It doesn't matter.

Because I'm smarter than all of them put together.

I'm better than all of them.

I'm better than him.

I'm the only one who knows the truth about him. So it's up to me to find a way to destroy him.

If they're going to escalate, I need to escalate. . . .

This isn't over. Not by a long shot . . .

I have many enemies in my life. . . . The Great Nemesis. The sheriff. Every clueless teacher and adult who's ever told me to "apply myself." Everyone who's ever not understood the point of my pranks.

But him . . .

He's the worst. He's the one I need to focus on. The one I need to destroy above all others.

After all — he's my archvillain. . . .

ACKNOWLEDGMENTS

Books don't happen in a vacuum.

Thanks to everyone at Scholastic for making this more fun than I ever imagined, especially Gregory Rutty and David Levithan (who refused to take "no" for an answer).

Also, thanks to my early readers: Faith Hochhalter, Allyson Lyga, and especially Eric Lyga, who sat patiently while I blathered on and on until the story assembled itself for me.

Last, I would be remiss if I did not thank the multitude of comic book writers and artists whose work I enjoyed as a child, and who quite thoroughly warped my mind to the point that I am qualified to write this series.